HUMMINGBIRD

HUMMINGBIRD

a novel

DEVIN KRUKOFF

© Devin Krukoff 2018
All rights reserved. No part of this publication may be reproduced, stored in a retrieval system, or transmitted in any form or by any means, graphic, electronic, or mechanical – including photocopying, recording, taping, or through the use of information storage and retrieval systems – without prior written permission of the publisher or, in the case of photocopying or other reprographic copying, a licence from the Canadian Copyright Licensing Agency (Access Copyright), One Yonge Street, Suite 800, Toronto, ON, Canada, M5E 1E5.

Published with the generous assistance of the Canada Council for the Arts and the Alberta Media Fund.

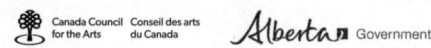

Freehand Books
515 – 815 1st Street SW
Calgary, Alberta T2P 1N3

Book orders: LitDistCo
8300 Lawson Road   Milton, Ontario   L9T 0A4
Telephone: 1-800-591-6250   Fax: 1-800-591-6251
orders@litdistco.ca   www.litdistco.ca

Library and Archives Canada Cataloguing in Publication
Krukoff, Devin, 1976-, author
      Hummingbird / Devin Krukoff.

Issued in print and electronic formats.
ISBN 978-1-988298-37-5 (softcover).--ISBN 978-1-988298-38-2 (EPUB).--ISBN 978-1-988298-39-9 (PDF)

      I. Title.

PS8621.R79H86 2018   C813'.6   C2018-902947-1
                                             C2018-902948-X
Edited by Rosemary Nixon
Book design by Grace Cheong
Printed on FSC® recycled paper and bound in Canada by Houghton Boston

For Raina Jean, the bravest little girl that I know.

All time is all time. It does not change. It does not lend itself to warnings or explanations. It simply is.

—Kurt Vonnegut, *Slaughterhouse-Five*

CHAPTER ONE

When the Connors moved out, I felt like I should have been consulted, or at least warned. I didn't know them in the traditional sense. We'd never spoken. I'd only gleaned their names from the buzzer outside the front entrance and the occasional piece of stray mail. But we'd been living in adjacent units for three years, and in that time our routines had gradually synchronized. I ate when they ate, slept when they slept, pleasured myself when they pleasured each other, spent so much time with my ear against the wall that my neck had a permanent crick. Our abutting bedrooms gave me intimate access to their lives, and not just their sex lives. From my mattress on the floor, I could hear every word they exchanged in bed—muffled but clear through the flimsy drywall and insulation. Whether they were making weekend plans or squabbling over money or wondering if they'd ever manage to conceive a child, I was listening. When they eventually got pregnant, I was the first to hear the news and raised a glass to the wall. For the first time in my adult life, I was almost happy. I had a book in print. A place of my own. A growing family to vicariously enjoy. From my balcony, I could almost see the ocean. The disorder in the apartment was useful, or familiar at least. I was accustomed to the dishes in the sink and the empty liquor bottles on the counters. I didn't mind navigating towers of second-hand paperbacks or kicking through piles of old shirts and underwear on my way to the bathroom. It's true that my place could have been nicer or bigger, but it had the essentials: a sitting room, a galley kitchen, a bedroom, and a four-piece bath. As for all the neighbours, I appreciated the sounds of them going about their lives—a spoon rapping against a pot, a body shifting in a bathtub, a vacuum cleaner grinding. People shouting, laughing, fucking all around me. I might not have spoken to any of them directly, but we communicated in other, more subtle ways, and I took comfort from the notion that we were part of the same community.

Of course, I wouldn't have wanted to actually live with any of them. In the past, whenever I'd been forced to room with strangers, I'd avoided the common spaces as much as possible. I never had trouble renting, as people sensed I would be a quiet tenant, but they inevitably came to resent how little they saw of me—holed up in my room for days at a time, pissing into empty pop bottles, eating from cans I'd stabbed open with a knife. They might not have known the lurid details, but they knew enough to get nervous. When I could finally afford a place of my own all that pressure to assimilate, to be *normal*, disappeared. If I wanted to be alone, I could be alone. All I had to do was slip a monthly cheque under the superintendent's door.

The Connors' departure changed everything; not all at once, but gradually, through events that hardly seemed connected at the time. They cleared out in the early morning, while I was still sleeping, having made no mention of their plans in earshot of the common wall. By the time I woke around noon—hungover, disoriented—a new tenant was lugging boxes down the hall. He looked old and unwell, with melted features, unkempt hair, and yellow jaundiced eyes. After watching him haul a television past my spyhole, I stepped onto my balcony and sent out a psychic ping but received nothing back, no glimmer of where the Connors had gone, no idea why they'd abandoned me. The day was bright and calm, the neighbourhood quiet. Not even the pale man—a shut-in who lived on the top floor of the low-rise across the way—was stirring. I lit a cigarette and scanned the sky for birds, not noticing that my new neighbour's balcony door was wide open until it suddenly crashed shut.

"No consideration!" the old man shouted from the opposite side of the glass.

I looked at the cigarette in my hand. I'd been smoking on that balcony for years. The Connors had never complained. I considered shouting this at the old man's door, or slamming my own door by way of response. Instead, I dropped the barely smoked cigarette into a glass of water and gingerly retreated into my apartment. The ceiling creaked as someone upstairs moved from one room to another. A toilet flushed and human waste rushed down through a pipe in my wall. I sat down with my laptop. An arrow became a hand, the hand became a cursor, and soon I was deep in the machine. I touched icons and windows swelled open. Message boards filled with sympathetic voices. My stress levels gradually diminished as I leapt from website to website, following a familiar winding path through Reddit and YouTube and Twitter to a celebrity news site, where every piece of gossip felt essential. By the time the light started fading in the windows, I'd all but forgotten the new neighbour. Then a hard craving for nicotine pulsed through my body and drove me over to the common wall. The old man was thumping around in his unit, moving furniture from the sound of it. I looked at my cigarettes. Only one thing could trump that compulsion. I went back to the laptop and touched a bookmark in a corner of the screen. A pixelated door appeared. An age verification button shaped like a keyhole. I clicked on the keyhole and was presented with a number of coloured doors. I selected the pink door and found myself in an actual pink room. Onscreen, a girl with red hair lay on a pink bed, looking straight into my eyes. She couldn't have been older than twenty, wearing a cut off T-shirt and low-slung jeans. Her name, a banner at the top of the screen informed me, was Jasmine.

Jasmine touched her breasts. She touched her face. She popped the button on her jeans and gave the camera a mischievous smile. Her eyes flicked from her webcam to the comments being left by users like myself on a little scrolling window beside the video feed:

Shake it bb
show yr pussy
RU HORNY???
PLZ SHOW YR PUSSY

There were eight of us lurking on the periphery of the pink room, our faceless avatars displayed alongside the comments, my alias—Midsummer Knight—at the top of the list, a little crown beside my name identifying me as a power user. I knew most of the girls on the site, but had never seen Jasmine before. I didn't contribute to the comments, content for the moment to watch.

After a minute, Jasmine leaned forward and typed: *hey midnite, how r u?*

My face grew warm. My fingers hovered over the keyboard.

Hello, I typed back.

i'm lonely, she wrote. *wanna go priv8?*

I composed and deleted several replies without sending them. Someone asked to see Jasmine's ass and she wagged her behind at the camera, proving that she was a real person sharing this exact moment in time with us, a person who, for a price, would be willing to do real things to her body, show what we asked her to show, touch where we asked her to touch.

Next door, the old man had gone quiet. I went to the bathroom and came back with a roll of toilet paper, checking the drapes to make sure they were shut tight.

Jasmine was still onscreen, the lurkers going on in their usual vein.

PUSSY PLZ!!!
so beautiful
I will come for you now...
    She sat back on her haunches and played with her hair, trying not to look bored. My finger stroked the touchpad. I double clicked and my credit card went through automatically. The other lurkers disappeared and the scrolling posts were replaced by a blank chat window with a blinking cursor. Jasmine gave the camera a sly smile and leaned forward.
hey midnite
    Hello, I typed back.
i had a feeling about you
    Did you?
mmmmm. where do you want to start baby?
    A little conversation.
    Disappointment flickered across her face, as if she'd rather have jumped straight to the show.
what do you want to talk about?
    I don't know, I admitted. I'd done this plenty of times before but felt strangely self-conscious, as if the camera feed went both ways, and Jasmine could see me as well as I could see her.
    Where are you from? I asked.
hollywood.
    I chuckled, knowing that the colour-coded rooms (I pictured them joined by a common hall, like cells) were in my city, a twenty-minute walk from my front door. They might not have advertised this fact on their website, but the information hadn't been hard to find.
    I decided to play along.
    What's the weather like in Hollywood?
hot, she wrote back with a grin. She was lying on her belly with her legs folded up behind her, ankles crossed
    What do you do in your real life? I asked.
real life?

When you're not on here. Do you have any hobbies or anything?
let's see...i like having sex, watching porn...
I laughed and shook my head, determined to break through, to make her real. *What about your family? Do you have any brothers or sisters?*
She stifled a yawn. *nope.*
I stared at the screen for a minute, not knowing what else to say.
so what do you do for a living? she finally asked.
I'm a writer
wow that's exciting
No, it isn't.
sure it is
I'm sorry, I wrote. *I'm terrible at this.*
at what?
Small talk.
so why don't we do something different?
Before I could answer, Jasmine swung her legs around and brought the rest of her body into view. She unzipped her jeans and flashed a triangle of panties—pink, like the walls of the room. She reached for her keyboard.
want me to keep going?
Yes, I wrote back, helplessly.
She shimmied her jeans down and kicked them away. I caught a glimpse of colour on her inner thigh—a tattoo, an iridescent wing.
are you hard? she wrote.
Yes, I admitted.
are you touching it?
Yes.
tell me what to do.

Afterwards, I closed the laptop, flushed the toilet paper, and paced in front of the closed drapes. The need for a cigarette had returned, stronger than ever. I'd just taken out my pack when someone knocked at the door. I didn't move. The knock came again, three firm raps, and I eased over to the door on the balls of my feet. Through the warped lens of the spyhole, I saw the superintendent's tight perm, the unforgiving slot of her mouth. She knocked again, her knuckles just inches from my face. I kept as still as possible, breathing through my mouth, aware of the tacky residue of semen on my stomach. She had the key to every apartment in the building. I pictured them on an iron loop at her waist, dozens of perfectly notched invasions. I rested my hand on the doorknob. The superintendent lifted her fist to knock one more time, then paused, as if sensing danger on my side of the door. She gave a small shake of the head, then turned and passed out of sight.

When she was gone, I sank down to a crouch, my grip on the present moment weakening. The air in the apartment rippled and I found myself on a carpeted floor, looking up at my father's delighted face. In his hands was a puppy the size of a well-fed gerbil. "Found her in a dumpster," he said, grinning as if he'd conjured the creature from thin air: a blind, deaf thing with a pulsing sucker for a mouth.

"It's all right," he said. "You can hold it."

I shook my head emphatically.

Dad laughed and dropped the animal in my lap, going off to look for my sister. The thing looked eyeless, tiny legs pistoning like parts on a windup toy. Its claws stabbed me, got traction in the folds of my shirt and propelled it up to my face, where it latched on my chin and attempted to feed. I flung the creature away with a shriek. It hit the wall with a decisive thump, just as my father and sister came back into the room.

"Jesus!" Dad yelled, scooping up the squealing puppy. "What is *wrong* with you, Felix?"

My apartment jerked back into focus. I could still smell the old house, still feel the thick carpet under my feet. My legs ached and I stretched them out on the laminate floor, wondering how long I'd been squatting there. Long enough for it to get dark. The hairs on my forearms quivered. I sensed Mathilda hiding somewhere in the apartment. Not the puppy I'd thrown that day, but the dog she became, a thick-necked, broad-chested animal who threatened anything that passed through her visible zone of dominion—a jogger, the mailman, a plastic bag animated by the wind. A humming insect swerved around my head, leaving me slapping at nothing. I heaved myself up and walked stiffly to the window, sparkles shooting from my knees to my toes. I listened for the Connors out of habit, missing their soft mutters, their careless laughter, their headboard tapping rhythmically at my wall. In the lit windows of the low-rise across the way, everyone was staring at a screen. My body strained for nicotine the way a submerged lung strains for air. After one last glance through my spyhole, I threw open the door and hurried to the stairwell, jogging down three floors to the back entrance of the building. The door closed heavily behind me. I fumbled with my lighter. Flame hit paper and I took a long and gratifying drag, then walked off quickly through the parking lot, making a moving target of myself to discourage anyone from talking to me. At the street, I kept going, mothlike and fluttering, heading instinctively for the brighter lights of the downtown shopping district. Individual strangers approached on foot and I felt myself drowning. But as the crowd thickened, my discomfort grew almost tolerable. I ducked into a twenty-four hour café, where I ordered a small coffee in a quavering voice and carried my cup to an isolated table beside one of the broad windows looking out onto the street.

This was what normal people did. They went out. They bought coffee.

I lifted my cup, but my hands were trembling so violently I had to set it back down without taking a sip. Outside, men dressed like boys and women dressed like hookers surged through the streets, mingling like dangerous tides. Two middle-aged men in ball caps and school jackets burst into the café, laughing. I hunkered over my cup as they ordered sandwiches, then sat down at the table next to mine. I pretended to look out the window, a hard tremor settling in my core. If I turned my head, I was certain I would find them staring at me. I was just considering what to do if they attacked, when my attention shifted abruptly to the view outside. A familiar figure was moving towards the window. She looked different out on the street, younger somehow, in an oversized sweater with the hood pulled up, but there could be no doubt who it was. Jasmine. She met my eye through the glass and I could tell that she felt herself recognized, or was aware, at least, of the possibility. Then her eyes flicked away and she passed out of sight.

"Go," one of the men at the next table muttered.

I glanced over, but neither one of them was looking at me. I stood up so fast that I nearly knocked over my coffee and headed for the door. Jasmine was at the end of the block, her hands jammed into the pockets of her hoodie. I followed at a safe distance, passing clusters of pedestrians with night-blurred faces. After a couple of minutes, Jasmine jaywalked across a busy street and joined a small crowd at a bus shelter. I crossed at a light, then doubled back and came up on her from behind, my eyes on the back of her head. She was smaller than I would have guessed from what I'd seen online, with the compact build of a gymnast. She looked down the street at an approaching bus and I saw her face in profile—heavy eyeliner, upturned nose, a small well-defined mouth. The bus pulled up and she climbed on nimbly, as if weighing nothing at all. A strong pair of invisible hands shoved me through the door, and I fumbled through my pockets for change. Jasmine was sitting alone near the back. I paid the driver and walked past several empty spots to her bench. She'd taken the window seat, leaving the aisle free.

I hesitated a moment, then sat down beside her. She sighed and tilted her legs deliberately away from me as the bus started moving again. I tried not to think about her shaved pubis, the hummingbird tattoo on her thigh.

The bus rounded a corner and I exercised all the muscles in my lower body to counteract the subtle forces pulling us together. She opened her handbag and took out a book. I glanced over, my anxiety briefly eclipsed by shock. She was reading *my* novel, the one I'd published two years before—my title on the spine, my name under her hand. If she'd turned to the last page, she would have found a black and white photograph of me standing beside a tree, squinting unpleasantly at the camera. I thought back on the last twenty-four hours, the string of events that had led up to that moment. It was no coincidence. It meant something. I could see that she was well into the book, and leaned in as much as I dared, wanting to know what page she was on, the exact paragraph.

"Good book?" I asked. My mouth was dry and the words came out all wrong—a click followed by an explosive *puhh*.

Jasmine tilted further away, the book (my book!) open in her lap. She was ignoring me by listening to me. Suppressing a wild laugh, I cleared my throat and repeated myself.

"Is that a good book?"

Jasmine looked around at the other passengers, looked outside, looked everywhere but at me.

"The reason I ask," I went on in a halting, shaky voice, "is that it's mine. Well, not *mine* exactly, but—" Jasmine snapped the book shut and stuffed it into her bag. She stood, and when I didn't immediately make way, she gave me a look of undisguised loathing. I muttered an apology and got up, allowing her to pass. Our bodies met for a moment (her elbow, my abdomen) and she carried on down the aisle. I sat down but she remained on her feet, holding a metal pole and staring straight ahead. When she alerted the driver that she wanted off, I stayed where

I was. The puppeteer that had manipulated me onto the bus had abandoned me, my strings gone slack. The neighbourhood out the window looked rundown and neglected, with drug deals happening in front of shuttered pawn shops. Jasmine got off and started walking. The bus kept pace with her for a moment before leaving her behind. An old woman across the aisle stared at me, as if I'd sprouted mandibles and feelers. I moved over to the window and the lingering heat from Jasmine's seat rose to meet me. I looked out at the darkened street, wondering what bus I was on, and where it would eventually take me.

» » »

The next day, I found a sleepy-looking girl with bleached hair performing in the pink room. The site was up twenty-four hours a day, with the girls working in shifts, taking coffee breaks as they would have in any other job, the live feed going dark whenever one of them disappeared with a paying customer. In the light of day, my humiliation on the bus felt like a simple misunderstanding, something Jasmine and I would laugh about when we got to know each other. I kept the laptop open, puttering around the apartment, making sure the screen was always active and pointed my way. Every time I went out to the balcony for a cigarette, the old man slammed his door. In the low-rise across the way, the pale man drifted from window to window, like a shark in an aquarium.

By late afternoon, the slamming was starting to get to me. A sarcastic brunette with short hair had replaced the blonde girl in the pink room, gesturing at the camera lewdly, almost mockingly, as the other users tried to provoke her into flashing them. I opened a parallel window and played game after game of solitaire until my right ear suddenly shut off, ghostly fingers sliding through my brain. A distinct, almost holographic image suggested itself between my eyes and the laptop screen: a small, dimly lit room, reproduced art on the walls, an open book in the foreground. A hand appeared and turned a page. Jasmine's hand. My words funneling into her mind. The vision faded. Next door, the old man was either coughing or laughing. Shaken, I went to the kitchen to scrounge something to eat. When I came back, Jasmine was on the screen. My heart sped up as she singled out my avatar with a friendly hello. I had the feeling that her handbag was just out of sight, my book nestled inside like a favourite pet. I didn't return her greeting, the medium feeling inadequate for what I had to say. As Jasmine's shift wore on, she disappeared with paying clients from time to time and I waited patiently, knowing that they meant nothing to her. We had the deeper connection.

Around midnight, Jasmine sent a goodnight kiss to the camera before disabling her webcam. I changed into clean underwear and slipped a condom into my wallet. I could hear the low drone of the old man snoring next door and thumped the wall just hard enough to wake him. I filled a measuring cup with vodka and drank it quickly, like medicine, then checked the spyhole and stepped out of my apartment. By the time I'd made it down to the twenty-four-hour café, the alcohol was gently rocking me in its arms. I ordered a coffee and settled at the same table I'd sat at the night before, next to the window. A light rain started to fall. I leaped forward to the scene that was about to unfold: a moment of unease, my words coming out perfectly, her face growing thoughtful as she realized what I knew already, that the universe wanted us to be together.

It being a Sunday, hardly any pedestrians were out. The streets were wet and shining. I nursed my drink, eyes never leaving the window. By one o'clock I'd begun to feel conspicuous. By one-thirty, I understood she wasn't going to come. As I walked home through the cold drizzle, criss-crossing the street to avoid occasional pedestrians, my disappointment twisted back on relief. In retrospect, I couldn't imagine any realistic scenario in which my accosting Jasmine on the street ended well. Still, the next night I headed down to the café the moment she finished her shift. And the night after that. I could have gone directly to the building with the coloured rooms, but it felt important to wait for her in the exact spot I'd first seen her, as if that location alone held the power to render us visible to one another. Night after night, I travelled down to the café, and every time she failed to appear, I experienced the same bittersweet mingling of disappointment and relief. I didn't want to see her, I wanted the *possibility* of seeing her. The fact that at any given moment, she could have been thumbing through my novel was enough. I would watch her. She would read me. There was reciprocity there. Whether she knew it or not, we had a relationship, and it bound us together as surely as a solemn vow.

CHAPTER TWO

Soft music floated through the gymnasium—a pan flute mingled with rolling surf, the distant cry of sea birds. Mr. Taylor had dimmed the lights and was pacing between our exercise mats, reading from a script. "Picture a beach," he intoned. "The sun on your face. The warm sand beneath you. A gentle wind ruffling your hair…"

Someone in the gym snorted. Mr. Taylor ignored them and kept reading. Two feet to my left, Nikki Pederson lay breathing evenly—hands on her stomach, feet bare. To say that I liked Nikki would have been a wild understatement. She wore safety pins in her ears and sleeveless T-shirts printed with grinning demons and flaming skulls. She had big thighs and small breasts, and her hair—a 1980s frozen waterfall—gave her at least three inches on me. Shuttered away in my room, masturbating into gym socks, I mainly thought about her mouth: how it looked when she laughed, or chewed gum, or smoked outside in full view of the teachers.

"Above you," Mr. Taylor read, "the sky is filled with colourful balloons. Those balloons are your restless thoughts. Wave goodbye to them. Let them float away…" He paced between the mats, frowning at the paper in his hand. "Wonderful. Now I want you to relax every muscle in your body, starting with your feet…"

Nikki flexed her toes.

"That's right. Let all that pent-up tension go. Now relax your ankles..."

With every named part, I grew increasingly tense, a map of Nikki's body unfolding as he moved from calf to knee to thigh. When he came to the genitals—when he actually *named* them—not one of the Grade Nine students around me made a sound. I was having trouble breathing. Nicki shifted on her mat. I didn't so much want to have sex with her, as I wanted to smash into her, to be pulverized by her.

"Be *in* the moment," Mr. Taylor read. "This moment of perfect stillness..." He let the waves play for a few minutes, then stopped the boom box and turned on the lights, giving us a minute to collect ourselves. Nikki stood up and stretched like a cat, arms up, butt out, drawing the attention of every heterosexual boy in the class. Even Mr. Taylor was watching her, his usual gruff manner returning as he sent us off to the lockers. I picked up my shoes and carried them past the girl's change room, seeing just enough to know that it was a fundamentally different space: lavender walls, gleaming white floors. In the comparatively dingy boys' locker room, I sat on a bench in front of my slate-grey locker and made the walls disappear. In my mind's eye, most of the girls in the next room were changing quickly, as if ashamed of their bodies, but Nikki stripped fully naked and strolled to the showers, pausing just long enough to glance over her shoulder and give me an inviting smile.

"Felix."

I looked over at Mr. Taylor, standing by the door.

"Get a fire under your butt, son."

I was alone in the locker room. The other boys had scattered. I looked at my watch. Chemistry class was about to start. I hauled on some jeans and hurried back out into the empty gym, where I ran into Nikki emerging from the girls' locker room, her hair wet, her mouth lacquered with purple lip gloss. Our eyes met. In some parallel universe we were wrestling on the gymnasium floor, our clothes blown from our bodies, students and teachers gathered in the bleachers to watch. She wanted it as badly as I did. I couldn't have been carrying all that desire alone. But of course, Nikki didn't look the least bit excited to be sharing the empty gym with me. She held me up for the briefest moment, like a shirt from a sale bin, then tossed me back down, her indifference absolute.

A glowing screen appeared in front of me. Suddenly, I wasn't standing anymore, but sitting in front of my open laptop, watching a woman do something creative with a large purple dildo. She looked uncannily like Nikki. I set the laptop aside, my head pounding. I'd fallen so deeply into the past that it took me a moment to regain my bearings. I raided the cupboards for painkillers and returned to the computer with a reckless dose of Tylenol dissolving in my stomach. A puzzled emoticon sat in the middle of my screen. I refreshed. Nothing happened. I restarted the entire machine but the coloured rooms had gone dark. My watch alarm went off, reminding me that Jasmine's shift was about to start. I tried to access her site in twenty different ways without success, my headache growing steadily worse, in spite of the drugs. At one in the morning I drank my vodka and headed downtown. The café was empty. I took my usual spot by the window, nursing my drink until one of the baristas came over.

"Waiting for someone?" she asked.

I blushed and shook my head. The girl had three studs in her lower lip, her head shaved on one side. She reached into my eyes and rummaged around in my heart, fingering the contours of my secret. I got up without a word and walked stiffly to the door, understanding that I would never be able to go back.

The next day, Jasmine's website was still down. I went to the bathroom and stared at the mirror for a long time before deciding I should eat something. My cupboards were empty, the fridge bare. I moved to the balcony and lit a cigarette, grinning fiercely to myself when the inevitable slam came. The smoke took the edge off my hunger, but I soon found myself back in the kitchen, opening and closing cupboard doors. There was no getting around it. I had to go the store.

    I took down my last bottle of vodka and finished it without measuring, then knocked the wildly protesting voice out of my head with three firm blows from the heel of my hand and made my way to the bus stop at the end of the street. A woman in a headscarf sat on a bench a few steps away, joggling an infant in her lap. The second hand on my watch moved incredibly slowly. I tottered on the curb, feeling as if I were standing on a diving board, an empty pool yawning beneath me. My chest hurt. I put my hands in my pockets to keep them still. I wanted to scream at the woman on the bench to stop looking at me. Eventually, the number six bus pulled up and I forced myself to climb on, finding an empty spot near the back. I looked out the window, seeing Jasmine everywhere: on the sidewalk, on the street, in the windows of passing cars. My fellow passengers scrutinized me mercilessly, and I cupped one hand to the side of my face to shut them out. The massive form of the supermarket appeared and I grabbed the cord on the wall and stumbled off the bus. The automatic doors whisked open. I crossed the threshold and a subtle change in air pressure confused my inner ear. The ceiling yawned above me, cross-hatched beams dotted with sinister black cameras. I struggled to dislodge a grocery cart from a jammed-up line until a teenaged boy in a blue vest yanked one out for me. "Thank you," I muttered and pushed the cart deeper into the store. One of the casters seized up every three steps, making a terrifying grinding noise. As I rolled past a wall of blaring cereal boxes, the pain in my chest intensified, migrating to my back and spreading across my shoulder blades like wings. The fluorescents added a fourth dimension to my fellow shoppers, rendering them hyper-real, bristling with whiskers and pimples and bloodshot eyes. I snagged items off the shelves at random—mayonnaise, sunflower seeds, raspberry-flavoured Kool-Aid. Every box or can that found its way into my hand involved a decision I didn't feel equipped to make. I grabbed spices that I knew I'd never use, abandoned produce in the wrong bins, forgot, then remembered, then forgot, to look for toilet paper, doubling back repeatedly, to the consternation of foreign-looking employees. And all the while, Jasmine haunted my peripheral vision, slipping out of view every time I tried to look at her directly. The alcohol burned out of my system. The workers exchanged secret codes over the PA and gathered behind glass display cases in the deli and the bakery to watch me. After three passes of the checkout lines, I approached a surly cashier who slammed my things into plastic bags, while I stared at a spot on the counter, tics fluttering and jumping all over my face. With four bags in each hand, I stepped out of the store and found my bus just pulling away. I slumped and trudged over to wait for the next one. How, I wondered, had things gotten so difficult? I'd made it through high school and several years of university. I'd held normal jobs, worked alongside other human beings, slept with at least five different women. But the world had gradually forced me out, the way the skin forces out a sliver of wood. And now that I'd been rejected, I had no way of finding my way back.

    A low-frequency pulse hit my ear and I looked up, expecting to see a helicopter, but the sky was empty. The next bus arrived, and I climbed on with difficulty, setting my groceries down and folding into myself—eyes shut, head against the vibrating window. The soft darkness pulled me down. I opened my eyes in the back seat of a station wagon. Stars out the window. A bright racing moon. My sister was sleeping across from me, a large dog on the seat between us. In the front, my father gripped the wheel with one hand and a Styrofoam cup with the other. I stared at the back of his head, sensing that he wasn't my father at all, but a stranger wearing my father's body, and that he was taking us somewhere unspeakable. The painted lines on the highway faded and vanished. The darkened fields we'd been driving through turned to water. The stranger caught my eye in the rear-view mirror, the lower half of his face illuminated by the glowing lights of the console, and I covered my mouth with both hands to keep from screaming.

Something jostled me and I raised my head.

I'd just missed my stop. I grabbed at the cord and quickly gathered my things. An orange fell out of one of my bags and rolled down the aisle. No one picked it up. On the walk back to my building, I thought about that orange. I hadn't bought oranges. In fact, I couldn't remember buying half the things bulging out of my bags. Another bus roared by. The sky went grey. Tiny flecks of rain hit my face. I struggled to control my breath, letting myself in the back door and lurching up the stairwell two stairs at a time. I'd nearly reached my floor, when I ran into the superintendent heading in the opposite direction. She gave a brief cry of surprise, her hand flying up to her chest.

"My goodness, you nearly gave me a heart attack!" She looked at the bags in my hands. "Doing some shopping?"

I nodded and gave an inane laugh. The superintendent was in her early fifties, a fair bit older than myself. From my vantage point, I had a clear view of her sturdy calves and several additional inches beyond, up the hem of her skirt. That she'd made occasional appearances in my masturbatory fantasies suddenly felt significant. "I was actually hoping I'd run into you," she said. "I've been trying to track you down for weeks. I was starting to get worried…" She seemed to realize how that sounded and gestured broadly. "We're a family here. We have to look out for each other…In any event, I'm sorry to have to tell you this, but we've had a complaint. It seems your new neighbour, Mr. Colombo, is extremely sensitive to smoke. Now I understand that this might be a small inconvenience, but I wonder if under the circumstances, you might consider indulging your habit elsewhere. Down in the parking lot, perhaps?"

The handles of the plastic bags cut into my fingers. My forearms strained with the weight of the groceries. I considered letting them go, watching them tumble down the stairs.

"He has a puffer," she explained. "Normally, I wouldn't ask, but it's a health issue."

"No," I said quietly, but firmly.

The superintendent smiled quizzically, as if she'd misheard me. Before either of us could say anything else, new voices echoed in the stairwell and two men in jogging shorts came trotting down from the floor above. I forged ahead with my groceries, noting the sharp tang of hand cream and the warm air pushing out of the superintendent's lungs as I sidestepped past her.

Half a minute later, I was back in my apartment, breathing hard, staring out through the spyhole, the bolt and chain thrown. I turned on the lights and looked around the room. Something was different. The curtains across the balcony door were open. I wouldn't have gone shopping without closing them any more than I would have neglected to lock the front door. It was more than habit. It was a compulsion. I strode across the room and saw the pale man at his window, arms at his sides, jaw slack. I swept the curtains shut, leaving my groceries by the door. It was all happening again. The paranoia. The terror. Something thumped the floor in the unit above, and I ducked dramatically. I went over to the laptop and opened it with trembling hands. I hit Jasmine's bookmark, wanting to see her, needing to see her, but the site failed to load as usual.

I refreshed. Nothing changed.

"Fuck!"

I navigated to a search engine and punched in keywords, anything I could think of.

stripper webcam Jasmine pink
I scrolled through the results: dozens of websites with hundreds of women, some even sharing her name, but none of them could give me what I needed. I tried again.
redhead webcam hummingbird tattoo Jasmine
Nothing.
I attacked the keyboard.
fuckfuckfuckfuckfuckfuck
Dusk was approaching. I sat in the semi-darkness, listening to the neighbours. A couch spring expanding. A knife scraping a plate. A suppressed cough. Sound after sound bombarded me, a steady crashing overriding them all, like someone pounding on a garbage can with a bat. I clapped my hands over my ears, and still the noise bled through. On my laptop screen, the search engine was waiting. I leaned forward and typed two final words, as if the machine itself might hear me and respond.
Help me.

CHAPTER THREE

From the empty glass in my hand, I concluded that I needed another drink. I went into the kitchen, and paused, looking at the bottle on the counter. Wine. I never drank wine. Just then, keys rattled in the door, and a woman with curly black hair blew into the apartment, all hectic and dishevelled.

"Sorry," she said. "Traffic was heavy."

She dropped a bulging paper bag on the counter and gave me a distracted kiss before rummaging in the cupboard for dishes.

I stared at her.

"Everything all right?" she said.

"I...I'm not sure."

The woman was on the heavier side, wearing jeans and a white peasant blouse. She moved through the apartment like she owned it, touching things, disturbing them. She unpacked the Chinese food, set two places at the table, and looked at me. "Aren't you going to sit down?"

I joined her at the table, and she began heaping food onto my plate. Stir fry. Egg rolls. Ginger beef. "So, you'll never guess what happened to me today."

I nudged an unfamiliar vegetable with my fork.

"I met Spencer Ford," she said.

"Who?"

"Spencer Ford! The poet."

I shook my head.

"*I Dream a Hidden House?*"

"Um......"

"Well, it turns out he lives down in South Harbor, and his Golden's a chewer. Shoes, electrical cords, furniture. Anything he can get his mouth on..."

I smiled and nodded, scraping the walls of my mind for traces of this woman. That we were dating seemed obvious from her tone (and the fact that she had a key to my apartment), but while she felt eerily familiar, I had no distinct memory of her. Whoever she was, she didn't expect much of a contribution from my side of the table. After telling me how she'd worked with Spencer Ford's dog, she described all the other animals she'd visited that day, from a yappy chihuahua to an anxious Irish wolfhound named Jack, whose owners she'd come upon in their backyard, squabbling over a half-built gazebo. Rather than minding her own business, she'd waded in between them to moderate the affair. The way she told the story, the couple welcomed the intrusion, confiding in her, speaking through her to one another, as if to a therapist. She heard them both out before informing them that the gazebo wasn't the real problem. The real problem was that they weren't having enough sex.

I nearly choked on my barbecue pork. "You said that?"

She'd segregated her food into neat piles, none of them touching, and begun to clear them away, one by one, counter-clockwise from the top. My own plate was a mess of fried rice, vegetables, and animal parts.

She shrugged. "It was obvious. I'd seen them before and they did everything a good couple was supposed to do. Teased each other, finished each other's sentences. But there was one important thing missing."

"What?" I asked, interested in spite of myself.

"They never touched. Well they touched, but they never *touched*. I'm talking love-touching here. There's a kind of touch—on the wrist, the shoulder, wherever—that signifies genuine intimacy." She reached out and grabbed my hand. "Like that. A touch that says I see you. I recognize you. I don't take you for granted."

Had I been pressed to put a word to what she was doing it would not have been "love-touching." Her grip was actually a bit painful. She burst into tearful laughter to recall how the chagrined couple had admitted that she was right, that maybe they did need to give their love life some attention. The story ended with the three of them sipping lemonade on the porch, then setting about building the gazebo together.

She set her fork down and looked at me expectantly.

"Well," I said after a moment.

She sighed, then got up and walked over to the sliding door. "I'm sorry I bored you."

I shook my head. "I wasn't—"

"We can't all have lives as thrilling as yours, you know."

"I didn't—"

"I'm out there helping people, Felix. Making a difference. You know, sometimes I just want to—" She broke off. "Oh my god!"

"What is it?"

"Come over here! Come here right now!"

I hurried over, not seeing anything unusual. The parking lot. The low-rise across the way. "There." She pointed. "On the top floor. Is he … ?"

The pale man was sitting in his apartment, looking at something out of sight, his hand in his lap, moving rhythmically.

"Yes," I said. "He is."

"Oh my god!" she laughed, covering her mouth.

"We shouldn't be watching him," I said.

"He's sitting right by his window."

"I'm sure he doesn't know we can see him."

"I'm sure that he does."

"Can you close the drapes, please?"

She rolled open the sliding door and shouted: "We can see you! Hey! We can see you!"

The pale man didn't seem to hear, or to care. The intensity of his arm increased and he arched back, then slumped.

"Oh," she said, her voice softening. "Oh, that's so sad."

"Can we close the door now?"

"He looks like he's about to cry."

"Close the damn door!"

She looked surprised, then her face shut down.

"I'm sorry," I said. "I don't know what's happening right now."

"What's happening,"—she closed the door and turned to me—"is that you think you're him. You're not, you know."

I forced myself to look at her. "Then who am I?"

She grabbed my hand and pulled me towards her. She was walking through a very different movie than the one I'd been cast in, a movie in which violins crescendoed as she kissed me hard. Our teeth banged together. Her tongue forced its way into my mouth. By the time we'd made it to the bedroom, my pants were down. "Wait," I said, but she put a hand on my chest and shoved. I fell back on the bed and my head hit the wall. She stripped quickly, then climbed onto the bed and roughly put on a condom. My socks were still on, my pants around my ankles. I stared at her in confusion, physically aroused, yet terrified as she climbed on top of me and guided me in, bending me back at a painful angle and slamming her full weight down on my body, using one hand to stimulate herself. I moaned in pain and she moaned in pleasure. Her hand became a blur. Her body shuddered. She tensed, making a low keening noise, then collapsed, breathing hard against my neck.

"Did you ... ?" she panted.

"Yes," I lied.

"Wow. Oh, wow. That was something. Wasn't that something?" She lay with her elbow on my diaphragm, wisps of hair irritating my face. Next door, I could have sworn I heard the old man applauding. When she finally rolled off, I disposed of the empty condom, disheartened to see that she had no intention of leaving. I didn't care who she was anymore. I just wanted her gone. I lay back down beside her and shut my eyes. After a minute, she put a hand on my chest. "Felix?"

I made a humming sound, pretending to be half-asleep.

"I want to take you shopping tomorrow," she said.

I opened one eye. "Why?"

She shifted up onto her elbow. "You're a famous author. You should look the part."

"I'm not famous."

"Stop being modest."

"I'm not being modest. I'm not remotely famous."

"You will be soon. We just need to work on your presentation. No one's going to listen to you if you're dressed like...well, I'm sorry, but like a homeless person. You might get away with rumpled. But sloppy won't get you anywhere. And your hair." She pawed at my hair, smoothing it straight back. "I think I like it like this."

I shut my eyes again as she rubbed at a spot on my arm with her thumb. "I mentioned you to Spencer Ford today. He gave me the name of an agent. Maybe you could get in touch."

"With Spencer Ford?"

"No, silly. The agent."

The spot on my arm felt raw, as if she'd rubbed off the first few layers of skin. The next time she said my name, I didn't answer. She sidled up close and roped her arm around me. I took deep regular breaths, afraid she'd start talking again if she knew I was awake. After a few minutes, a vague pain settled into my legs. I tried to ease away but her hold on me tightened. I lay perfectly still, waiting. The pain was becoming unbearable. Just when it seemed that she'd never let go, she flopped onto her back and began to snore.

I quietly moved to the darkened living area. She'd left her purse by the door, a handmade-looking thing holding a small assortment of personal effects: lipstick, loose change, business cards for the Well-Heeled Dog Trainers. The name on her driver's license was Kim Penn. My math put her at twenty-nine years old. In a little hidden compartment on the side of her purse, I found an unmarked vial of pills and a neatly folded note from a fortune cookie that read, *Your future will exceed your expectations.* I carefully put everything back, then patted my own pockets, surprised to find that not only did I not have any cigarettes, I had no *desire* for a cigarette. I sat in the dark for a while, then opened my laptop and squinted in the sudden light, the search engine greeting me like a stone idol in a cave. I reached for the keyboard and stopped, feeling oddly tentative. I'd forgotten how to interact with it. I didn't have a thing to say.

» » »

When I was eighteen years old, Dad drove me halfway across the country and dropped me outside the twin dorm buildings of the West Coast College with a look of barely concealed relief on his face. Within a few weeks, a strange disorganization had crept into my life. I'd ask my roommate, a Vietnamese exchange student named Henry, if he'd seen my watch or my keys or my calculator, and he would give me a brief, horrified look, as if I'd offended not only him but his entire family, before shaking his head and returning to his homework. By the winter term, I was losing blocks of time. At first, I attributed it to fatigue, but as the semester wore on, the gaps widened from hours to days. Sometimes it was relatively easy to catch up on what I'd missed. Other times I'd be utterly lost, with no one to fill me in but Henry, who'd begun to regard me warily, as if the structure of my face were changing in some small but perceptible way.

I learned to adapt to these leaps in time, accepting them as a normal part of my existence, a phenomenon that came and went, with no discernible pattern. But Kim's appearance in my apartment marked the biggest shift I'd ever experienced. I'd lost more than a month, long enough for us to have not only met but fallen into something of a routine. Two or three times a week, she'd stop by after work, talk about herself for an hour, then drag me to the bedroom—dominating me, my arousal a joyless autonomic function that I'd actually started to dread. When I woke the next morning, she'd be gone. I couldn't say just how we'd met, but she had definite ideas about who I was, or more precisely, who she wanted me to be, bringing me uncomfortable shirts from upscale second-hand clothing stores, leaving moody compilations in my CD player, forcing me to watch films that were either infuriatingly experimental or pointlessly disturbing. I'd only published one book (which I doubted she'd even read), but she possessed an unwavering faith in my abilities as a novelist and assured me that she'd been working hard to increase my visibility around town, promoting my "brand" in her sprawling network of clients and friends.

When she insisted that I write something new, I started work on a romance novel about an English professor and an exotic dancer just to spite her. I wasn't writing about Jasmine. I was writing *to* her, letting her know that I was still out there, that I would wait for her. The message couldn't have been clearer. These are your instructions. Find me.

Kim, meanwhile, was spending increasing amounts time at my apartment—reorganizing the kitchen, learning my pincodes, introducing a houseplant and an incense burner to the bedroom. Like any shrewd invading general, she befriended the locals, chatting with my neighbours when I wasn't around, dispensing dog-related advice. But it wasn't enough. She wanted more. She wanted *me* to change, to accompany her out into the world. When she showed up one evening with tickets to a play at an amateur theatre, my anxiety levels instantly spiked.

"I have work to do," I said, edging towards my laptop.

She pulled a yellow pill vial from her purse and rattled it in front of my face with a grin.

"What's that?"

"Diazepam."

I gave her a blank stare.

"Valium," she clarified. "I got them from a vet friend."

"You want me to take dog meds?"

"It's the same stuff they give humans." She shook out two pills. "It's fine. I've taken them myself."

The pills had heart-shaped holes in them, as if they were meant to be strung onto a little girl's necklace.

Kim went over to the sink and came back with a glass of water. "Open."

She tucked the pills into my mouth. I swallowed them and grimaced. She rubbed my back. "Good boy. Now go lie down. I'll come get you when it's time to head out."

To my surprise, the Valium helped. I went to the theatre. I watched the performance. I applauded with everyone else. When we got home, I felt invigorated, inspired to create. I shuttered myself in the bedroom with my novel and wrote for twelve hours straight, ploughing my way to the end of a first draft. The moment I stopped typing, Kim tapped on the door.

"How's it coming in there?"

"I think I'm done," I said.

"Really?" She peered over my shoulder. "Did you save it?"

"Of course."

"Did you back it up?"

"No, but—"

"Which file is it? This one?" She reached over me to plug in a jump drive and copied the manuscript onto it. "There. I'll print out a hard copy at my place."

"You don't need—"

"I don't mind." She slid the jump drive into her purse and looked at her watch. "Wow, is it ten o'clock already? I'd better get going. Talk to you later, Felix!" She breezed out of the room and the front door slammed. I closed my laptop, feeling as if I'd just handed my life savings over to a stranger. I wanted the book back, but incredibly, had no idea how to find her. Kim had always been the one to initiate contact. With no phone number or address to refer to, I was going to have to wait.

Three agonizing days later, Kim called from a coffee shop, a strumming guitar and chattering voices in the background.

"I'm here with David," she informed me.

"Who?"

"David Cavendish. Spencer Ford's agent? I showed him your book."

"What book?" I asked, confused.

"The one about the dancer."

It took me a second to understand what Kim was telling me. "You showed my manuscript to someone else?"

"I didn't think you'd mind."

"It's a rough draft!"

"He's upset," I heard her tell David.

My hand tightened around the phone. I had no idea what David looked like, but pictured a thin man in suspenders and dark-rimmed glasses, smirking as he noted clumsy passages, bad grammar, and inconsistent character names—all of it permanently saved on the hard drive of his brain. There was no way to undo the damage, short of murder. I saw myself storming the coffee shop with a gun, a kitchen knife, a pen—rammed into his esophagus, my words gushing from his body and pooling all over the floor. Kim was talking again.

"I missed that," I said, putting my free hand to my suddenly throbbing temple. "What did you just say?"

"Sorry, it's loud in here. David says he wants to represent you. He has some publishers in mind. He expects you'll get a good advance."

"Advance?" I said weakly, wondering if she was making fun of me. My first book hadn't made any money at all. I was actually in debt to the small press that had published it. At any moment, I expected her to explode with laughter and hang up the phone.

"Hold on," Kim said. "I'll pass you over to David. He can explain better than I can."

Before I had the chance to protest, the phone changed hands and a new voice came on the line, a hearty voice that managed to sound both enthusiastic and condescending at the same time. "Hello, is this Felix?"

"Yes."

"Felix, this is David Cavendish, from the Whitson Agency. How are you today?"

"Fine."

"Glad to hear it! Glad to hear it! So I had a look at this manuscript of yours. *The Pole*? It's really quite good. Sexy but not tawdry. Suspenseful in places. The ending actually moved me a little. Anyway, there's a solid market for literary erotica right now and I'm fairly confident we can find a home for this. I was hoping we could get together in person and hammer out the details. Assuming you haven't signed with anyone else."

I couldn't seem to find my voice, still seeing the pen embedded in his skinny neck, his body sprawled on the ground, hemorrhaging language. A low drone came from the line, as if something was interfering with our connection.

"Hello?" David said, sounding very far away. "Felix? Are you there?"

» » »

"How much do you love me?"

The question came out of nowhere. I was sitting in a chair in the middle of the living area with a towel around my neck. Kim had borrowed some clippers and a pair of scissors from a hairdresser friend and was giving me a much-needed haircut. "When we first met," she said, trimming around my left ear, "you were like a raggedy old dog that had been kicked around its whole life. Look at you now. All cleaned up. Getting out of the house. You have to admit, I've been good for you." She moved in front of me and started on my bangs, scissors snipping uncomfortably close to my eyes.

"No?" she asked, when I didn't answer. "You'd think that after everything that's happened—the book deal, the advance—you'd be just a little bit happy."

"I'm happy," I said, automatically.

"Could have fooled me."

Our faces were inches apart, her eyes on my hair. She moved out of my line of vision, trimming around my right ear. "I'm not expecting a proposal or anything," she said. "But a little gratitude would be nice...I can give you the number of a florist if you like. Hell, I can call them if you need me to."

Her snipping was getting increasingly aggressive.

I didn't know what she wanted me to say. I hadn't asked for any of this. Her presence in my life had been one big imposition, and now I was supposed to thank her?

"Do you ever think about what life's like for the rest of us?" she demanded. "People who don't have the luxury of throwing up their hands? We keep going, Felix. We make it work because we have to..." Her scissors grazed the back of my neck. "The tiniest effort, that's all I'm asking. Some help. A sacrifice..."

She'd stopped cutting. I could have lied to her, told her that I cared for her, that everything was going to be all right. Instead, I sat motionless in my chair, staring at all the cut hair on the floor. I wondered where the scissors were, if she was holding them in her fist, the way a person holds a knife.

Do it, I thought.

I shut my eyes and waited for the scissors to impale my neck, feeling her desire, knowing she was capable of it. Instead, she just sighed and started tidying up the back. A few last tufts of hair drifted to the floor, nearly weightless. When she'd finished, she brought a hand mirror around to the front of the chair and held it under her chin so that my face appeared to be embedded in her chest. I ran my fingers through my hair, surprised by how well the cut suited me.

"Like a new man," I said, softly.

CHAPTER FOUR

"I told you not to look at me," Chad muttered as he ground my face into the snow. "Didn't I tell you not to look at me?"
"I didn't!" I gasped.

Nearly twice my size, Chad straddled me like a professional wrestler, bending my arms and legs in ways they weren't supposed to bend, as if I were an action figure he'd gotten for Christmas. None of the other kids on the playground moved to help, watching with solemn faces as he forced my head back down. I had no idea what I'd done to deserve such a beating (I hadn't looked at him—quite the opposite), but Chad was enjoying himself now, putting on a show for the kids who were shielding us from the playground monitors. "Who wants to see it?" he asked them. "Who wants to see Fee-lee's tiny dick?"

"No!" I hollered, fighting to break free.

But Chad had already rolled me over and jerked the front of my sweatpants and underwear down with his free hand. The moment the cold air hit my hairless genitals, I went slack, like a rabbit that knows it's about to die.

"Oh my God!" he laughed. "Anyone got a magnifying glass?"

The school bell rang and he released my waistband with a snap. The kids all ran for the doors and Chad trotted after them, throwing a wistful look over his shoulder, as if at a project he looked forward to finishing. By the time I got back to class, I'd decided exactly how I was going to kill him. I'd grab an aluminum bat from the equipment room and wait for him outside the back door of the school. The instant he stepped into the light, I'd swing. The bat would connect with his face and he'd hit the ground. No. One blow wouldn't do it. It would take at least three. One to the face. One to his defensively raised arm. A third to the back of the head. When he was down, I'd adjust my grip and focus on his upper body—hammering him in the chest, the stomach, his stupid broken face. Other kids would pile out, watching in stunned silence as Chad sobbed and howled at my feet. One or two might run back inside for help, but I wouldn't let up. I would keep on swinging until someone forced me to stop.

At noon, I looked up from my workbook. I'd been so caught up in the fantasy, running it over compulsively in my mind, adding satisfying little details and flourishes (the angle of his smashed nose, the faint wheeze of his failing breath) that I had absolutely no idea what I'd been doing for the last hour and a half. Math, from the look of it. I tucked the book into my desk and grabbed my coat and gloves from my locker. The routine required no thought. I would be home in ten minutes, eating a sandwich in front of the television. My breath leaped from my body as I stepped out of the school, the murderous film still looping through my head. I was making gestures now, jerky little half-swings, muttering through my teeth as I stared down at Chad's swollen, battered face, his trembling hands rising in one last plea for mercy. I beat them down. This was happening. It was real as anything I'd ever done. The surrounding houses faded, as if *they* were the things being imagined. I didn't see the sheen of black ice on the road ahead. I had no awareness of the teal blue Chevy Nova bearing down on the intersection I was about to step into. In that particular moment, I wasn't seeing anything but blood, or hearing anything but my own frenzied screams.

The world flickered.

I reared back in my chair, trying to make sense of the scene coming into focus around me. Kim and two strangers, sitting across from me at a small table. Stuttering lights. Bass thudding up from the floor. Across the club, a woman in a G-string stood on an elevated stage, moving her hips broadly as she danced. Kim yelled to be heard over the music, saying something that sounded like "money" to a bald man beside her who appeared to have fallen asleep. When I recognized the other person at our table as the superintendent of my building—garishly made up, in a tight black dress—I nearly shouted in surprise.

You all right? Kim mouthed at me.

I tried to stand up, but couldn't catch hold of the room's spinning edges. The glass in front of me was filled with a green liquid that glowed under the black lights of the club. My mouth tasted like hard candy and ash. As the stripper on the platform sleepily removed her G-string, the superintendent's foot bumped up against mine under the table and stayed there. Kim started to laugh. She laughed until tears rolled down her face and the superintendent began giggling along with her. The bald man jerked awake, his eyes falling on me, and he too started to laugh. Up on the platform, the stripper was spinning around the pole, fully naked. Only when my stomach began to hurt did I realize that I was laughing harder than any of them, and none of us, our faces twisted grotesquely, as if in pain, seemed to be able to stop.

"Where was your head?" Dad shouted. He was pacing around my bed in what looked like a hospital room. Tubes ran into my body at multiple points. Plaster immobilized my elevated leg from calf to thigh. My sister sat in a chair across the room, hugging her knees and eyeing me narrowly. The last thing I remembered was hoisting a bloody bat and drawing a bead on Chad Temple's barely recognizable face. I couldn't imagine how I'd ended up in the hospital, but Dad's tone left no doubt that I had only myself to blame.

"I'm sorry," I croaked.

Dad stopped pacing. "Sorry? Jesus Christ, you don't have to be sorry, Felix. You have to be careful. Next time you might not be so lucky."

"What—"

"A car ran you down," Eileen said, with evident pleasure.

"Came out of nowhere," Dad added. "That's what the driver said. Waltzed right in front of his car without looking. If he'd have hit you at a slightly different angle…"

I frowned at a crack in the ceiling. I had no memory of the accident. What I remembered was murdering Chad. Of the two events, that was the one that felt more real just then, more relevant.

Eileen made an unimpressed motorboat sound with her tongue. "Does Felix have to go to school tomorrow?"

Dad shook his head. "Oh, he'll be out of school for a while after this."

"No fair."

"Something's happening," I whispered.

The crack on the ceiling was expanding, new fissures opening and spidering out, as if under intense pressure from above.

Dad looked up, then back down at me, confused.

"Cracks…" I said.

Eileen laughed and bounced in her seat. "Felix is going crazy!"

I shrieked as a dark shape punched through the plaster, the pointed tip of something enormous. Dad put a hand on my chest. "Whoa there! Hey! We need some help in here!" He hammered the call button beside the bed.

I flinched as two more booming impacts came, making a hole the size of a car tire in the ceiling. I tried to get away, but Dad held me down as Eileen looked on with horrified delight.

"What's happening?" Dad asked a nurse who'd arrived in the room.

A massive black eye appeared in the hole and another scream ripped out of my chest. I clawed at Dad's arm.

"What's wrong with him?" he shouted at the nurse, who advanced on me with a syringe. She plunged something into my IV line and I sagged, still terrified but fading.

"Just a bad reaction to the morphine," the nurse said.

"No," I moaned, fighting to stay awake. "It's..."

I surfaced in the dim living room and looked around wildly. This was new—being hammered back and forth in time like a paddleball. Kim was cutting her toenails beside me on the couch. I flinched as one hit me in the face. "Sorry," she grinned wickedly. "Did I get you?"

On the TV, a couple was French kissing, tongues grappling.

"What day is it?" I asked Kim.

She laughed. "Wow. You really do need to get out more."

"I—"

Another jump, like one roll of film spliced onto another.

I was back on the playground, surrounded by kids in shorts and T-shirts, the snow turned to grass. Chad leaned against a wall by the basketball courts, but he wasn't really there. He couldn't have been. Not after the way I'd attacked him with that bat. I limped over and he walked off in the opposite direction, pretending not to see me. "Chad!" I called to him. "Hey, wait up!" He disappeared into the school, and I followed him into the bathroom, where he wheeled on me, looking almost afraid.

I grinned at him. "You can do it now. I don't mind."

"This again?"

I limped closer. "Come on. Do it."

His jaw flexed. "No."

"Do it!"

He hauled back and punched me in the mouth.

I smiled, tasting blood. "Do it again."

He slammed me against the bathroom wall and jerked my arm behind my back. I gasped as something popped in my shoulder.

"There! Happy?" He shoved me to the floor.

I got back up, my hurt arm dangling. I had earned that pain. I *enjoyed* it. But it wasn't enough.

"I—" My voice was weak. "I need you to do it again."

Chad stepped back, teeth bared, tears in his eyes. "What is *wrong* with you, man?"

"Just one more time."

"Get away from me!"

"Please..."

"I said, get away!"

"It's he-re!" Kim sang as she lugged a heavy-looking cardboard box into the living area. I tried to look like I knew what was going on, like I wasn't expecting to be hauled off again to some random moment from the past. I was shocked that we were still together. I couldn't have been acting remotely normal. She dropped the box on the coffee table in front of me. "Well? Aren't you excited?"

"Uh..."

She sighed and tore open the box, scattering Styrofoam popcorn as she pulled out a hardcover book. On the front, between my name and the title, a man and woman in silhouette straddled opposite sides of a stripper's pole. Kim turned the book over in her hands. "It's beautiful," she said. "Isn't it beautiful?"

"Wow," I said dutifully, recalling the bizarre strip club scene with the superintendent and the bald man. "Hey, um...have you seen my building manager lately?"

"Nancy? No. Why?"

"No reason," I muttered, unsettled by the fact that they seemed to be on a first-name basis. Kim hauled out more books, piling them on the table. It was like some dark ritual. The books. The scented candle juddering on a side table. Kim insisted that I hold one and I turned to the first chapter. Pressure filled my head. The opening lines felt as if they'd been written by a stranger. I read on, but none of it was remotely familiar. Not the pace or the cadence or the setting. Even the names of the characters had changed. I closed the book, invisible talons slicing the air in front of my face.

"It's all different."

"Uh-huh," Kim said, distracted by the book in her hands.

My head felt incredibly heavy. I stood up and the claws became wings, bursting into sight and vanishing all around me. I made my way to the bedroom, holding the walls for support, while Kim hummed softly to herself on the sofa. The moment I sat down on the bed, the phone rang. Kim picked up and spoke in a low voice, making plans that somehow involved me. The harder I listened, the less I could hear.

"*Where was your head?*"

I jerked around. Dad's exasperated voice had come from right beside me, as if through a hidden speaker in the wall.

"Shut up," I whispered back. My head was compressing, collapsing on itself until it emitted a thin whine of protest, before abruptly expanding, filling the bedroom with space, widening it into a maze of books—alphabetized stacks spanning out in every direction from the cluster of reading tables I was sitting at. The other tables were empty. My knapsack sat on the floor by my feet. I tried to focus on my statistics textbook, but something pulled my eye to the folded newspaper on the next table. A grainy photograph of Chad Temple in a striped polo shirt and shorts, smiling a big unguarded smile, surrounded by kids with swollen stomachs and tiny arms. I reached over and grabbed the paper, feeling gravity slacken on my body as I read the accompanying article. According to the author, Chad had been working overseas for a Christian aid agency when he'd been murdered in an alley behind a youth hostel. Bludgeoned to death. The motive for the killing wasn't known, though investigations were underway. Towards the end of the article, a family friend testified to Chad's excellent character. "He didn't deserve this," were the friend's exact words. "He never hurt anyone in his life."

A vague pain radiated through my head. I folded the paper and surreptitiously tucked it into my knapsack, along with my statistics book.

As I left the library and crossed the busy campus, my headache swelled to a full-blown migraine. The fact that I'd found the article at all was remarkable. I hadn't seen Chad since grade school. I never followed the news. If I hadn't been studying at that exact moment, at that exact table, I'd have never known what had happened to him. Back in my dorm room, I sat on my bed and reread the article, looking for clues, some hidden pattern beneath the words. *He never hurt anyone in his life.* At those words, my humiliation in the schoolyard returned, fresh as ever, along with everything that had followed—my rage, my guilt. Two possibilities occurred to me, both of them equally insane, both of them strangely plausible. Either I really had murdered Chad in my childhood via some future proxy, or I'd simply foreseen his death, my mind framing the event in terms it could understand.

The door swung open and I stuffed the newspaper under my pillow.

Henry came in, looking surprised to see me. He gave me a terse nod and sat down at his desk with a thick Chemistry book. I pictured myself hoisting him out of his chair and lurching over to the window, our shared momentum carrying us through the glass and down to the paved courtyard below. He stiffened, as if receiving the image through an invisible cable.

To counteract the horrors going on in my head, I asked him the first thing that came to me. "Are you religious, Henry?"

It seemed like a reasonable question. We'd been roommates for two years and I hardly knew a thing about him. He remained quiet for a long moment before answering. "I'm sorry?" he said, still frowning at his book.

"I was just wondering if you're religious."

"No." He glanced over his shoulder. "Why?"

I shrugged. "No reason."

"Well, my mother is Buddhist," he said, carefully. "And my father is Catholic."

"So you're . . "

"A little of both, I guess."

"I see." I smiled what I hoped looked like an innocent smile, the image of us going out the window together lingering. It made no sense. I had no reason to want to hurt him. "So . . " I cleared my throat. "What are you doing this weekend?"

He returned his eyes to his schoolwork. "Studying."

"Oh. Okay."

I watched him vacantly for a while, as if he were a television screen, my consciousness and body peeling apart like two segments of an orange. Henry shut his book with a sigh and got up, saying he'd forgotten something in the computer lab. When he was gone, I looked at my hands, thinking about the tiny digits hidden in birds' wings. *Phalanges*. I closed and opened my fists. The usual sounds of the dormitory—a racquetball smacking a wall, an out-of-tune guitar, a peal of female laughter—were overlaid by a steady throbbing in my right ear. I rubbed at the ear, and the whole of my childhood rushed through my head, as if spun through an impossibly fast projector. The experience was over in seconds, accompanied by an odd suction and a swell of emotion so intense I could hardly bear it. Everything was there. Every sensory detail. Every lucid moment. I cried out briefly, as though in sexual pleasure, then lowered my hand from my ear, stunned not so much by the realization that my memories had been so meticulously archived, but that the archives were *accessible*. If I could find a way to tap into that frequency and slow down the film, I could relive my life, moment by moment. The notion should have been reassuring. But as I took the newspaper out again and looked at Chad Temple's smiling face, it brought me no comfort at all.

» » »

I returned to consciousness reluctantly, trying to swim back into a dream in which I'd been wandering through an enormous glass-walled hotel in search of my missing head. Sunlight pushed at my eyelids. I gave up and rolled out of bed. Kim was out in the sitting room, pumping her arms as she walked in place with headphones on. I sat down on the couch and stared at her until she took the hint and turned off her MP3 player. "What's up?" she asked.

I felt like I hadn't slept in months. One of my hands quavered uncontrollably, as if I'd had a stroke. "I think..." I said. "I'm losing my mind."

"Oh?" She started to walk again, leaving the sound off.

I told her everything, about the blackouts, the leaps in time, the jarring returns to the present.

Kim frowned, as if to say, *I'm listening*, but her gaze kept wandering off to a spot just over my shoulder. I was struggling to convey just how real the visions felt when she interrupted with an impatient flick of the hand.

"That happens to me all the time."

"What? No, I don't think you understand how vivid—"

"No, I get it."

"It's a sensory experience. I smell things. Feel things."

"Right." She looked at me like I was a naïve child, describing the most common phenomenon in the world.

"That happens to you all the time."

"Absolutely."

"But—"

She walked faster, her hand edging towards the MP3 player hooked over her waistband.

I shook my head. "Forget it."

The walls were slightly off-kilter, as if the apartment had been dismantled and hastily reassembled while I slept. I heard the faint rhythm of Kim's workout music start up again. There would never be a better time to end things. One simple, unambiguous statement and it would be over. But before I could say a word, a hard jolt brought me into a new space, a smaller, dimmer space lit by strings of Christmas lights. A naked, middle-aged woman sat beside me on a futon, smoking a joint and studying me with detached interest, as if she intended to paint me. Feeling simultaneously heavy and weightless, I tried to sit up. I'd never smoked pot before and was fascinated by the way one green light on the wall flickered whenever I asked it to. How the rhythmic song on the stereo had been skipping for the last ten minutes. Even in the dim light, even drunk and high, I could see that my companion wasn't beautiful. Her teeth were blocky and yellow, her stomach rolled with fat and sagging with age. But her pale green eyes had a trace of kindness in them, a glimmer of a real person, a person I might have been able to love.

"It's okay," she said.

A meaningless noise left my mouth and dissolved in the air.

"Don't fight it." She rested a hand on my arm. "Let it take you where you need to go."

We were both naked, but I couldn't remember having sex. I looked around for my clothes as the skipping song came to an end and another one started, a tinny synthesized melody against a slow driving beat. I tried not to panic about my complete loss of coordination, or the fact that someone else was crouched in a corner of the room. A boy. Arms wrapped around his knees.

"What is it?" the woman asked.

"He's watching us," I whispered.

"Is he?"

"Do you see him there? In the corner?"

She took one last hit on the joint and set it in a little ceramic ashtray, then wrapped a silk robe around herself and went over to the stove on the other side of the room. The burner clicked and she put a kettle on. "Tea?"

I shook my head, still watching the corner. All this felt familiar, like it had happened many times before. Chad Temple's face appeared over the small body.

"Do you know him?" the woman asked.

I nodded.

"Is that a good yes or a bad yes?"

"A bad yes," I whispered.

"Would you like me to make him go away?"

I nodded again, then flinched as she flipped a switch. Light flooded the room, thrown from a bulb on a wire. The dingy room had little in it besides the futon. In the corner, Chad had transformed into a step stool draped with a peach-coloured bra.

"Okay?" she said. The harsh light revealed the woman's thick makeup, her scarred hands, the stubble on her calves. But her movements were graceful, and she didn't seem the least bit self-conscious.

I wrapped a blanket around myself. "Okay."

The woman shut the light and came back to the futon. "How old are you, sweetie?"

"Twenty-four," I said, still watching the corner.

"Do you want to tell me your name?"

"I…No, I don't think so."

She shrugged. "Okay. Sometimes it's better that way."

Chad had reappeared, his adult head on the body of a child. "I'm still seeing him," I said. "Is that normal?"

"Who wants to be normal?"

"I do."

"Well, that's a shame."

All at once, I felt inexplicably sad. The marijuana amplified the emotion and the alcohol loosened my grip on it. I started to cry, quietly at first, but soon I was sobbing.

"Well, that's no good," the woman said. "Come here."

She gathered me into a hug and I leaned against her, choking back a rush of aimless grief. The woman stroked my hair, hushing me, and I sobbed into her chest until the kettle started to buck and whistle.

"I need to get that," she said, gently.

I dropped my head to my hands, sick and ashamed.

"Sure you don't want tea?" she asked. I shook my head and wiped my eyes. She brought her cup over and gave me a tired smile. "Where are you from, sweetie?"

My tears receded as abruptly as they'd come, leaving a cool blankness in their wake. I felt under the blanket for my clothes.

"Did you grow up around here?" she persisted.

"No. I ... Sorry, have you seen my pants?"

The woman smiled, as steam writhed above her cup. "You know, I wasn't sure if I should tell you this, but I went to that bar tonight looking for you. Not someone like you. *You*. And here you are, sitting on my couch. Isn't that funny?" She gazed at me intently. "We were like two magnets, sliding together..."

I had no memory of meeting the woman or making my way to her place. She seemed to have conjured me there, like a witch in a fairy tale. A cool draft swept over me and I shuddered. The step stool in the corner was just a step stool again. My limbs remembered how to move. I groped around the legs of the futon.

"What's wrong?" the woman asked.

"Nothing. I'm just cold."

"Why don't you have some tea?"

I nudged something furry under the futon and pulled my hand back. The kettle whistled again. I looked around and saw that the stovetop was empty. Fear pricked at my scalp. The woman muttered something about magnets, how stubborn they could be. She lowered her cup to the table in slow motion. The whistling grew louder, higher in pitch. Then in a flash, I was on top of her, wringing her throat with both hands as she flailed and clawed at my back, her face going dark. I jerked out of the vision. The whistling had stopped. I hadn't moved. The woman was still in the process of putting down her cup, but she looked stunned. Her free hand went up to her collarbone. "I think…" she said, "you'd better leave."

"Why?" I said. "What did you see?"

She got up and opened a door onto a narrow hallway.

"That's not me," I told her. "Whatever you saw, that's not who I am."

In the light from the hall, I spotted my clothes balled up under the futon and grabbed them, quickly hauling them on. "I wouldn't hurt you," I insisted, as if the woman had contradicted me. "These things, they just come. I don't know why…"

The woman remained at the door, saying nothing. I grabbed her by the arms and slammed her up against the wall. The scene collapsed. I was still standing on the opposite side of the room. I couldn't have possibly touched her.

"Hank!" she called, an edge of panic in her voice.

A thick-necked bald man appeared in the doorway. "Everything all right?"

"I want this boy to leave."

"You heard the woman," Hank said.

"I didn't do anything!" I shouted. "I didn't touch her!"

Hank stepped into the room and the woman stopped him with a hand on the arm.

"Look," she said to me. "I feel for you. I really do. But whatever you need, whatever you're missing, you're not going to find it here… So this is what's going to happen. I'm going to count to three and you're going to get the fuck out of my room."

"But—"

"One."
"I just—"
"Two."

I hurried past her into the hall, turning to ask, almost desperately: "Do you still want to know my name?"

"No," she said. "I don't."

She shut the door, leaving me alone in the hall with Hank, who shrugged and gave me a look that was not without sympathy. "Go home," he said. My eyes were stinging. I wove down the hall to the front door and half-fell down the stoop. The sidewalk was dry but I felt like I was stepping in puddles. I hugged a streetlight and patted my pockets. No wallet. No keys. I did a slow turn, squinting at the surrounding buildings. The effort of remembering what door I'd come out of was too much. I vomited on the street without warning. Two women in short skirts went "Ohhhh!" and cackled as they passed me by. I staggered to an empty payphone booth at the end of the block. Every number I'd ever committed to memory scrolled through my head as I picked up the receiver. After a long moment, I set the receiver back down. There wasn't a soul in the world I could have called for help.

CHAPTER FIVE

The apartment had never been neater: counters gleaming, the clutter gone, the recycling and trash in their designated receptacles. The previously bare walls had been filled with amateurish but original renderings of brightly coloured doors. The bathroom was spotless, a red toothbrush resting against mine in a glass on the sink. The bedroom was just as neat, dirty clothes in a hamper, the comforter on the bed, perfectly square. The telephone beside me rang and I picked up cautiously, with the tips of my fingers.

"Hello?"

"I'm on my way home," Kim said, as multiple dogs barked in the background. "Have you eaten?"

"Um…I'm not sure."

"Oh boy. I'll be there in half an hour."

Strangely apathetic, I sat half-dozing by the telephone until it rang again.

This time a male voice greeted me.

"Just a friendly reminder. Eight o'clock at the university."

"The university?"

"That's right. I assume you'll be leaving fairly soon? If you're taking a cab, remember to get a receipt."

I stood up to clear my head and bright spots bloomed on the wall.

"I'm sorry, who is this?"

"It's David Cavendish."

"The agent?"

"Ye-es."

"I'm sorry, I'm just a little...under the weather."

"Felix...You're not trying to back out on me, are you?"

"No," I said, surprised by the aggression in his voice.

"Good. I know it's not your favourite thing to do, but it's necessary. Two hours of your life and it'll be over. I'll find you when it's done."

I hung up and looked at my watch. The hands wobbled and tipped, before resolving at their fixed points. Six-thirty. I couldn't seem to wake up. I wanted to put on coffee, but the cupboards had all been rearranged. I gave up and stopped in front of the fridge. A dog-shaped magnet held an advertisement for a reading at the university auditorium, featuring me and a number of other authors. Before I could even think to panic, the door rattled and in came Kim, wearing dramatic makeup and a feathery looking skirt. Her smile fell when she saw me. "You're not dressed."

"Where are the coffee filters?"

"On the microwave. Why aren't you dressed?"

"On the *microwave*? How am I supposed to find them there?"

"Felix."

"What?"

"Why aren't you dressed?"

"I'm sick."

Her face darkened. She marched into the bedroom and brought out a pile of folded clothes. It seemed easier to obey than protest, so I stripped off my sweatpants and T-shirt and put on the collared shirt and slacks that she'd chosen. As she did up my tie, I stood with my arms at my sides, transfixed by the fleshy bud of her pursed lips, painted a jarring shade of red. She grabbed a sport coat and loafers out of the closet, then wet her thumb on her tongue and wiped at something on my right cheek. I suspected there was nothing there, that she was licking her thumb and wiping again, just below my eye socket, to prove some strange point.

"There," she said.

"I don't want to go."

She took me by the hand and dragged me out of the apartment. An impotent ball of fury swelled in my chest as we rode the elevator down to the lobby, but when we stepped out the front door, I held her hand tightly, grateful to not be alone. The sun had fallen behind the buildings to the west, the sky a dusky shade of blue.

"How many people are going to be there?" I asked, as a steady stream of cars rolled past on the street.

"I don't know."

"I can't do this."

"Taxi!"

"Please don't make me do this."

But she'd already flagged down a cab and was handing the driver a card with the event's location. In the back seat of the car, all the muscles in my stomach collapsed on a single stabbing point. "Kim..."

She extracted a pill caddy and a bottle of water from her purse. The driver watched us curiously in the rear-view mirror as Kim shook out pills of different shapes and sizes. I swallowed them all and she patted my leg. "Close your eyes. I'll see you in twenty minutes."

"I want to go home."

"Twenty minutes," she said, firmly.

I sat back and shut my eyes. My stomach lurched every time the car took a sharp corner. I was about to insist that the driver stop and let me out when a spigot in my chest twisted, and all the tension flooded from my body. I opened my eyes and looked at Kim. Whatever she saw in my face made her grin. "Better?" she asked.

I nodded, intrigued by the sensation of my head going up and down.

"Good. We're almost there."

The cab pulled up outside the auditorium and we climbed out together, no longer holding hands. The student at the door gave me an identity card and directed me across the foyer to the event organizer, a man with a long face and prominent incisors, who narrowed his eyes as we approached.

"Mr. Mallory?" he said.

"That's right," Kim said.

"Present," I confirmed, listing to one side and catching myself.

The man's upper lip twitched, exposing his front teeth and I snorted. His nose began to lengthen and I laughed out loud.

"He's fine," Kim said.

"I'm fine," I agreed in a strangled voice.

The organizer looked unconvinced. "Things will be getting underway soon," he said, tersely. "You'd better come with me."

The more suspicious he became, the more rat-like he looked. Nearly weeping with suppressed laughter, I left Kim to join the main crowd and followed him through a side door into the darkened auditorium, past a group of students watching a disaster movie on a small television. A building on fire. Stampeding men and women in business attire. A news ticker rolled across the bottom of the screen, and I realized that it wasn't a movie. Somewhere in the world, this was actually happening. The organizer kept me moving with a forceful nudge, steering me over to the wings of the stage, where he melted back into the shadows. A handful of authors were milling around, unaware that I'd joined them. From their subdued conversation, I gathered three things:

1. None of them had taken a cocktail of unknown psychotropic drugs on the cab ride over.
2. Armed rebels had just seized the American embassy in an obscure but strategically important Middle Eastern country.

3. The sleeve of my jacket was on fire.
I flapped my arm and the fire went out.
"Looks like a good turnout," one of the other authors observed. I smiled at her, before realizing that she was talking to the person next to me. For a brief moment, I was back in high school, raising my hand to Nikki Pederson in response to a wave that she'd actually—and *obviously*—directed at someone over my shoulder. The house lights dimmed and the emcee for the evening strolled out to the podium, dressed in black, his silver hair gleaming. As he began to speak, a hot wind blew across the stage and the spotlight became a sun, beating down through a smoky haze onto the shimmering face of the American embassy. Children with automatic rifles grinned down at me from the compound's high walls. A distorted voice crackled through a megaphone, reciting a long list of names before compelling me to approach the flaming building. I moved through a grove of smoldering trees. The embassy appeared to be constructed of cardboard and glue, smoke pouring from its windows. Inside, someone was either shrieking in pain or furiously playing an out-of-tune violin. I climbed the steps to the front door and gripped an ornate handle. Then everything went quiet.

The emcee was standing over in the wings. I'd replaced him at the podium.

Fainting would have been the logical thing to do, but I remained painfully conscious under the audience's collective gaze, my legs having lost half their muscle tone. The auditorium was packed. I looked over at the emcee and he made a frantic encouraging motion. I gripped the podium and leaned into the microphone.

"Hello."

My voice reverberated through the auditorium. The spotlight stabbed at my eyes. A copy of *The Pole* rested on the podium in front of me. Clearly, I was meant to read from it. "Okay," I muttered, thumbing through the book, or *trying* to thumb through it, as some prankster had glued the pages together. A quiet rage poured into my head as I struggled to pry the book open. I glared out at the crowd and they stared back at me without expression. I was about to hurl the book into their midst, when a familiar face came into focus in the front row. She wore eyeglasses, and her long red hair had been cut in a short, angular style, but I would have recognized her anywhere. The book in my hands cracked open. I looked down in surprise, then back up at Jasmine. She gave me an encouraging smile. I took a shaky breath and started to read.

There had been no good reason for Jeremy to weigh in on the Banister scandal.

The line was so unfamiliar that I read on with genuine curiosity.

He didn't know Ted Banister. They taught at different schools. Jeremy had nothing to gain by offering his point of view. But he had, and the moment he did, the dozens of apathetic young faces before him filled with interest. "To be clear," he said, walking it back a little, wondering how he'd segued from Madame Bovary to this, "Professor Banister's actions ought to be investigated. There's no doubt about that. But I can't help wondering if his suspension was a tad premature."

At the back of the room, a hand shot into the air. Jeremy's diaphragm clenched. He paced behind the lectern, eyes sliding over the athletic blonde owner of the hand. "There are multiple sides to every story," he hurried on. "In life as in literature, there are reliable and unreliable narrators. At the moment, we have one perspective. I think we'd do well to reserve our judgment until all the facts have been gathered—"

The girl's hand was still in the air, waving now. Jeremy threw a look at the empty spot where Madeline would usually be sitting. It had been nearly a week since he'd seen her. She hadn't responded to any of his recent texts. He was starting to feel desperate.

"These are dangerous times," he said, making eye contact with a few of the male students. "When the word of one individual can destroy a life, we should all be very concerned. A mere allegation—"

"Serious allegation," the blonde girl interrupted, no longer content to wait.

Jeremy looked at her. "I'm sorry?"

"It's a serious allegation. Not a mere allegation."

"Of course it's serious," Jeremy said. "I never disputed that."

"You could have picked any adjective. If someone was accused of murder, would you say they were mere allegations?"

"Perhaps not," he admitted. "But professional misconduct and murder are two very different things."

"Sexual misconduct," the girl corrected him.

"Yes, well. That is the allegation..."

Dark mutters rolled through the classroom.

"It isn't just one," a thin brunette in the front row said. "Three other students have come forward."

"Four victims," the first girl agreed.

Victims? From what Jeremy had read (and he'd been following the story closely), the professor had been involved in a consensual affair with one of his students. Inappropriate? Perhaps. But hardly criminal. As for the suggestive comments he'd been accused of making to students behind closed doors, it wasn't as if anyone had been physically hurt.

"I read that he'd been doing it for years," a third girl said. "The school administration had received multiple complaints and no one did a thing."

Several other girls nodded in solidarity. Jeremy felt himself losing control of the room. With Madeline in the picture, it was hard not to take all this personally. Of the hundreds (if not thousands) of students he'd taught in his career, she was the only one he'd ever slept with. It wasn't as if he'd gone looking for her. He hadn't known she'd be dancing at the Tiger Bomb that first night. He didn't force her to have a drink with him, or to come back to his apartment. It was true that she'd hesitated when he kissed her. And she could have been a little more enthusiastic in bed, but there had been no refusal, no insistence (or request even) that he stop. She'd called him the next day. She returned to his apartment on multiple occasions without coercion. From a legal standpoint, he was in the clear.

So why wasn't Madeline there?

"Bare minimum," one of the male students said—not the sort you'd expect: muscled and dim-looking, with a ballcap and football jersey—"dude should lose his job."

"And if the relationship with the student was consensual?" Jeremy shot back, realizing his mistake the moment the attention of the class swung back his way. In the silence that followed, only two sets of coordinates mattered, his spot at the lectern, and Madeline's empty seat. They knew. Every one of them knew what had been going on. He raised a hand in defense, although no actual accusation had been levelled. "I'm sorry," he stammered. "I don't mean to sound old-fashioned. But human relationships are complicated... I think we all need to take a step back and—"

A gunshot rang out in the auditorium.

I jumped and ducked behind the podium. No one else reacted. The audience members appeared perfectly calm. One of the other authors in the wings made an apologetic face and stooped to pick up a thick hardcover book. Meanwhile, someone in the audience started to clap, having evidently decided that I'd finished reading. The applause spread through the room, mounting to a polite level. In the spot where Jasmine had been just moments before, an old woman sat, pointedly not clapping. I ran my eyes over the audience, looking for some familiar face to hold onto.

The emcee emerged from the wings to thank me with what felt like an ironic bow, keeping me where I was with a firm hand on the shoulder. "Brief," he observed drily, "but suspenseful...Well! Before we let you go, let's see if there are any questions from the audience, shall we?"

The house lights went up a notch, revealing two or three raised hands, and an undergrad waded into the crowd with a microphone. I clutched my book, wishing I could have read more, unsettled by the tone of the writing, how unsympathetic the professor had been. Hardly the leading man I'd envisioned.

A girl with perfectly braided hair took the microphone and cleared her throat. "So...I picked your book up on a recommendation from a friend, and I wasn't entirely sure what to make of it. To be honest, it reads like an apologia for male chauvinism. Your professor spends half the book trying to convince us that he's not so bad, and the other half feeling sorry for himself after his life falls apart. As if he didn't bring it all on himself. And as I'm reading, I can't help wondering what you want us to feel. I mean, where do you stand on all this? Do you sympathize with the professor?"

I made a floundering gesture. Whatever the book had become, I hadn't set out to make any kind of political statement when I started writing it. I'd just been trying to reach Jasmine.

"It's...complicated," was all I could think to say.

"Actually, it's not. Either you identify with the professor or you don't."

The emcee's hand remained firm on my shoulder. I lowered my head, waiting for the next bullet to come. "If I might respond?" a faint voice called from elsewhere in the auditorium. I looked up with gratitude, as the undergrad carried the microphone over to a middle-aged woman in a red blazer. "Thank you. I don't mean to hijack the question, but I wanted to offer something of a counterpoint...Now I can't speak to how deep an affinity the author may or may not have with his protagonist, but I thought the choice you presented him with was rather unfair. It presumes the professor to be either a hero or villain, allowing no room for nuance. I regard him as something of an endangered species. An educated man of a certain generation who should know better but doesn't. But *why* doesn't he know better? That's an important question. You'll never know the answer if you don't spend some time unpacking his psyche."

The first girl wanted to speak again and the undergrad jogged over for her rebuttal.

"I'm sorry," she said, "I have no interest in the professor's psyche. Or any other part of him. There's a time and a place for complexity. A book written long after the Holocaust might have the luxury of humanizing Nazi soldiers. But a book written *during* the holocaust? It has the moral obligation to focus on the victims."

"But don't you see we can do both things?" the older woman protested when the microphone reached her again. "We can support the girl *and* regard the professor with circumspection. How else can we ever truly hope to understand?"

"You're wrong," the first girl said. "When you look at the professor, you lose sight of the girl. It's as simple as that. And the girl is screaming."

The older woman shook her head and sat down, apparently concluding that any further debate was pointless.

"A spirited discussion!" the emcee observed, leaning into my microphone. "Well, I think we have time for one more, if... Yes, back there. The gentleman in the black shirt."

The undergrad travelled up the stairs to an overweight man with a bushy white beard and a heavy metal T-shirt. He scratched his belly and peered down at the stage. "I'm just wondering if you're familiar with the tool known as emasculators. Veterinarians use them to castrate large animals. They resemble an oversized set of pliers, and they have a unique function... After the scrotum's been sliced open, they clamp the emasculators behind the young bull's testicles to sever the blood supply while crushing the spermatic cord." He squeezed a fist in the air to demonstrate. "At this point, the testicles can be safely removed. It isn't for the squeamish. There's some blood, but the pressure prevents hemorrhaging..."

"Excuse me," the emcee said. "I fail to see how this relates—"

"If you'll let me finish." The man glared over his shaggy beard. "Now the levels of pain for the bull are debatable. A local anesthetic is generally applied. But one thing is certain. The bull's temperament is irrevocably altered by the procedure. He grows smaller, more docile, more predictable, easier to manage, more...cowlike, as it were. Of course, the bull is not a cow. In addition to obvious anatomical differences, the animal would never be accepted by the other cows as an equal. But neither is the bull truly a bull anymore. Farmers understand this and give the animals an entirely new designation. They call them steers. And what, you may ask, is the function of a steer? To be eaten. That is all. To have any utility, the animal must die. One can't help but wonder if—"

"I'm sorry," the emcee said, "but we're running short on time. I'm afraid we're going to have to move on to our next author."

"Now hold on just a second..."

After a brief tug-of-war, the undergrad reclaimed the microphone, and the emcee removed his hand from my shoulder. The bearded man kept talking, shouting what sounded like "Resist!" from the back of the auditorium, until two forbidding young men in dark-rimmed spectacles went over to physically remove him from the room.

I followed my own path out of the auditorium, plodding over to the wings, where, on the small muted television, men in suits were wandering around in a daze, as if they'd lost something important. I retraced my steps to the foyer, where I found the organizer setting out refreshments and the students who'd removed the bearded man, looking grim. The bearded man was nowhere to be seen. The organizer impatiently directed me to a long signing table where a small pile of books awaited each author, along with a bottle of water and a cheap-looking pen. The young men paced around me like prison guards. Muffled applause drifted out of the auditorium. After a very long time, the side door burst open and the remaining authors bounded out, grinning like loveable criminals in a heist movie. They took their spots without acknowledging me, while the crowd filed through the main doors. Kim appeared and headed straight for the signing table, her lipstick framing a dangerous-looking smile. "Darling!"

"I need to leave," I said, quietly but urgently.

She glanced at the authors flanking me, then threw back her head and laughed. "You're so *funny*. Well, I'm going to go mingle. See you in a bit…" She strode off in the direction of the refreshment table. The authors on either side of me leaned ever so slightly away, as if from an offensive smell. People had begun to line up at the signing table. I was just considering how to make my escape, when I saw Jasmine again on the far side of the room, smiling faintly and looking around with interest. The crowd opened and closed behind her, bringing her inexorably closer to the signing table until she stood directly in front of me—my first novel, the one she'd been reading the night I followed her onto the bus, in her hand. She set the book down on the table and smiled, pleasant but distant, as she might have smiled at a cashier at the bank.

"Angela," she said.

"I'm sorry?"

It was the first time I'd heard her speak. I'd seen every inch of her body. She'd written the most explicit things imaginable to me. But up to that moment, her voice had been a mystery. She sounded older than I'd expected, more educated, her A's betraying a slight mid-Atlantic accent.

"My name," she said. "For the inscription."

"Oh. Right."

I'd always assumed that Jasmine was a stage name, but it had suited her. She didn't look anything like an Angela. I opened her book, distracted by the scent of something coconut-y drifting across the table.

"Do you—" My voice failed me and I cleared my throat. "Want me to say anything in particular?"

I watched her closely for a sign, some acknowledgment that we'd met before.

She shook her head. "*To Angela* is fine."

It occurred to me that she might not have even read my latest book, a book I'd written specifically for her. Given the degree to which it had been sabotaged, that could have been a stroke of luck. My pen hovered over the page. I was just working up the nerve to ask for her last name when Kim came galloping back over to the table with an incredulous look. "Angie?"

Jasmine turned to her with a smile that I would have murdered to have put there. "Kimmie?"

They squealed. They hugged.

"Oh my God!"

"I know!"

"Where have you—"

"Don't ask."

I sat with a strained smile, waiting to be introduced, but Kim seemed to have forgotten she even knew me. The friends linked arms and wandered over to the refreshment table, happily chatting. Kimmie and Angie. The whole thing felt strangely orchestrated, designed to cause me pain.

The authors on either side of me were busily signing books. Still holding Jasmine's copy of my first novel, I opened the front cover and wrote two words: *To Jasmine*. I underlined her stage name twice, then slammed the book on the table and headed for the exit. My vision blurred. My legs felt like they'd been hollowed out and filled with cement.

"Felix!"

The voice sounded so much like my father's that I froze, but the man coming at me through the crowd was more heavyset than Dad and closer to my own age, his neat goatee framing a wide, confident smile. David, my agent. He grabbed my hand and pumped it, radiating a minty, boozy smell. "What did I say? I told you you'd do fine, didn't I?"

I responded with a feeble shrug.

"Quite the interrogation they gave you up there," he chuckled. "They really come out of the woodwork for these things...So, where are you off to? Not leaving already, I hope?"

"I'm not feeling well..."

"Really! Well, before you go I have something I need to talk to you about."

Kim and Jasmine were huddled over by the coffee urn, laughing uproariously at some shared reminiscence. Kim met my eye across the room and leaned over to say something in Jasmine's ear.

I stepped towards the exit. "I really have to..."

"This'll only take a minute," David said, ratcheting his smile up a notch.

"Hel-lo," Kim said brightly, having left Jasmine to come eavesdrop on our conversation. Through a gap in the crowd, I could see Jasmine going back to the signing table to collect her book. Kim slipped her hand into the crook of my elbow, while David sucked his teeth for a moment.

"So..." he said, "it isn't that your book isn't doing well. It's doing fine, as far as it goes. But the people upstairs had hoped it would do..." He bounced his hands in the air, as if weighing a pumpkin. "Better. I've been told that you're not getting enough exposure. This reading's a good start, but they want more. Interviews. Festivals. Now I know how you feel about doing publicity..."

Jasmine had nearly reached my vacant spot at the signing table.

"Let go," I muttered to Kim, unable to move with her hand locked to my elbow.

"There are ways of dealing with these things," David continued. "Mindful meditation. Deep breathing. Pharmaceuticals."

I pried at Kim's fingers. "Let. Go."

Across the room, Jasmine picked up her book and turned to the inscription.

"Would you fucking let go already?" I shouted, jerking my arm free. The room went quiet. Kim stared at me with an oddly vacant expression, like a doll on a shelf. I put my eyes on the floor and headed for the nearest exit, not daring to look at Jasmine, or anyone else. No one tried to stop me. No one said a word as I reached the front doors and pushed out into the warm, dark evening. Orange halogens illuminated the empty street. The bearded bull expert was sitting on the grass. "Spare some change?" he asked. I backed away from him, power-walking down the sidewalk, then breaking into a run. The wind caught my tie and carried it over my shoulder. I passed the library and my old dorm building, sprinting now, past students in backpacks, leaving them to watch after me and wonder if they themselves had cause to panic in the face of this most ominous of sights: a well-dressed man running for his life.

CHAPTER SIX

After a long, disorienting moment, I understood that I hadn't, in fact, been buried alive. Weak light pushed under the door, illuminating the shapes of a toilet, a hamper, a wall-mounted sink. A band of pain tightened around my head as I hauled myself out of the empty bathtub and groped for the light switch, shielding my eyes from the sudden flood of brightness. Fruit flies darted all around me, dotting the walls, coating the damp towels on the floor. The toilet seat was up, the bowl flecked with vomit. I filled the sink with cold water and lowered my face into the pool. At the count of ten, I reared back, making glancing eye contact with the creature in the mirror: a pale, bloated thing dragged up from the bottom of the sea. The one lit bulb above the vanity mirror hummed.

I opened the door and found that fruit flies had colonized the entire apartment. Takeout containers and empty bottles and cans had exploded through the living area. A pile of unopened bills lay below the mail slot. Kim's door paintings were gone, along with her clothes, her CDs, her books—any evidence of her presence in my life having been erased. I picked up the phone, but if I'd ever learned Kim's number, I'd forgotten it. After listening to the dial tone for a moment, it occurred to me to push redial. The line rang.

Kim answered warily, as if fairly sure who'd be calling. The moment I heard her voice, I started to cry. She sighed. "You have to stop calling here."

"I'm sorry." My voice was thick with tears.

"Jesus, Felix! Don't do that. Don't cry at me."

"I'm *sorry*."

"It isn't fair. What you're doing right now is not fair."

"I miss you so much," I sobbed, and as I said the words, I realized they were true. When we were together, I'd disliked everything about her. But now that she was gone, it seemed that she'd been just about perfect. "What can I do?" I moaned. "Tell me what to do."

She exhaled slowly. "What, exactly, do you think you miss about me, Felix?"

"Everything."

"Can you be a little more specific?"

I came up with what felt like a safe answer. "Your eyes."

"My eyes," she said flatly.

"Yes."

"What colour are my eyes, Felix?"

I could hardly picture her face, let alone her eyes.

"I…"

"You have no idea, do you? What about my middle name? My sign? My favourite movie?"

"Tell me," I said. "I want to know everything."

She gave a hollow laugh. "It's too late, Felix. Stick with whatever caricature of me you had. It'll be easier that way."

"Why are you doing this?" I wailed.

"Me? You did this. You're the freaking ringmaster."

"That's not true!"

"Look, I have to go. Can we say goodbye like adults? I really don't want to have to hang up on you again."

"Can't we just—"

"Goodbye, Felix."

"Wait!"

"For fuck's sake!" She took a long breath and exhaled. "Okay...Do you remember my friend Shauna? The therapist? I can give her a call if you'd like. I'm sure she'd fit you in."

"I don't need a therapist."

"Really. Then what do you need?"

"Another chance."

"Felix, we don't even like each other!"

"That's not true!"

Someone laughed in the background on Kim's end, a high-pitched, tinkling sound.

"What was that?"

"What was what?" Kim snapped.

"That laugh. Is someone..." I sat up straighter, my extremities buzzing. "Oh god. She's there, isn't she? She's sitting right next to you."

"Who?"

"Jasmine."

"*Who?*"

"Angela."

"*Angela?* What does she have to do with anything?"

The woman laughed again, derisively, it seemed to me.

"Ask her what's so funny," I said.

"Felix..."

"Ask her! Ask *Jasmine* what's so funny. Or better yet, ask her about the pink room. I'll bet she hasn't told you about that."

"Oh, wow," Kim said. "You're actually crazy..."

"You can't do this," I sobbed. "You can't just breeze into someone's life, then walk away like nothing happened."

"As a matter of fact—"

I was done listening. I shouted and hurled the telephone across the room. It bounced off the wall and skittered along the floor. The impact almost broke the receiver in two, but somehow it didn't sever our connection. I could hear Kim's tinny voice coming from the open line on the floor: "Felix, what just happened? Are you there?"

I sat on the couch, coolly watching the phone for a moment, before leaning down and gently severing the connection. My finger was still on the disconnect button when the phone rang a few seconds later. I lifted my finger. "Kim?"

"Felix?"

Not Kim after all, but my sister, sounding concerned.

"Eileen?"

"What's happened?"

"What do you mean?"

"You've been crying. I can hear it in your voice. Did someone die?"

Another wave of grief hit me and a sob broke out of my mouth. "Oh god, she left me, Eileen!"

My sister sighed, all sympathy draining from her voice. "Oh."

"I don't know what to do!"

"This was a girlfriend, I take it?"

I curled on the couch, clutching the broken phone to my ear. "I can't live without her!"

"I'm fairly sure that's not true."

I cried like an overtired child, ignoring Eileen's halfhearted attempts to console me.

"Well, I'm glad no one's dead," she said, once my crying jag had passed. "I had a terrible dream. That's why I called you. I was feeling superstitious. I thought something might have happened."

"What kind of dream?"

"It was about Mathilda. She was older. Grey around the muzzle, like she was towards the end, you know? Anyway, I'm back in the old house and I've got this paper cut on my arm. A tiny little slice that's hardly bleeding at all, and Mathilda comes over and starts to lick it. I want to push her away, but I don't because I feel like she needs it. So I'm holding my arm there and she's licking and licking. And the more she licks, the bigger the cut gets, until she's not just licking my arm, she's licking *inside* my arm. Lapping, like a dog drinking water from a bowl. And then, God, I'm feeling sick just remembering this, then she starts to nibble. Delicately, at first, with her front teeth. I'm still not doing anything to stop her, because it doesn't hurt. I could move if I wanted to, but I'm fighting to keep still. I'm letting it happen. Even when she starts tearing off little chunks of skin and meat—not aggressively, but gently, looking very peaceful while she's doing it—even then I don't pull away. Because it's my obligation to feed her. But when I see my own arm bone hiding under all that gore, I can't hold still anymore and I start to scream. I start to fight...That's when I woke up."

"That's horrible," I said, forgetting Kim for the moment.

"Like I said, it was a nightmare." She yawned. "There was no way I was getting back to sleep with that image in my head and Peter snoring beside me, so I got up to make myself a cup of tea. I saw your number on the fridge. I figured you'd be around."

I thought it over. "I'm the dog."

"How's that?"

"You said the dream made you think of me. I'm the dog."

"Um...no. I was actually thinking—hang on a second." She half-covered the phone to say something to her husband, then came back on. "I should get going. I've got an early morning tomorrow. I just wanted to make sure you were okay."

"I hated her," I said.

"Excuse me?"

"Kim. When we were together, I hated her and she knew it. But everything's different now. I'd do anything to get her back. It's like she changed me somehow. She put all this *need* inside me."

My sister was quiet for a long moment. "You know," she finally said, "you might want to talk to someone. Like a professional."

My hand tightened around the receiver. "That's what Kim said."

"Well, she's right. I hope you're not harassing her."

"What?"

"Don't play dumb. You know what I mean."

"I...Why did you call me again?"

"I was worried. But you're okay. So." She kept saying it, as if repetition would make it true. "Have you talked to Dad lately, by the way?"

I made a vague noise, unsure just how long it had been.

"You should give him a call."

"Why?"

"You just should. Listen, it was good to hear your voice. I really need get back to bed..."

We hung up after promising to talk again soon, neither one of us meaning it. Ever since she'd moved to New Zealand, we'd been like strangers. All the same, I felt better for having talked to someone. I put the phone down and it rang again almost immediately. I answered without thinking.

"Hello?"

"You bastard."

"Kim?"

"I thought you'd done something to yourself. I was about to call the police."

"I'm sorry," I said, surprised and touched.

"What is *wrong* with you?" she shouted.

"I just...had a problem with my phone."

"*A problem with your phone?*"

"The line cut out."

"The hell it did. I heard background noise. I thought you'd fucking killed yourself!"

The louder she got, the calmer I became. Her anger was irrelevant. She cared. That was all that mattered. As she continued to harangue me, someone knocked at the door. I carried the phone over and found the superintendent on the other side of the spyhole. I held the phone against my chest, watching her. She knocked two more times then gave up and went away. I put the phone to my ear again. "Kim, listen..."

"No, you listen!" she said, her voice breaking. "You're sick! You're a sick human being, Felix!"

I laughed, without knowing why.

"This is funny to you?" she yelled.

"No," I moaned, laughing so hard my stomach hurt.

She sputtered for a moment, then grew dangerously calm, uttering four words, with the intensity of someone laying a curse: "Never. Call. Me. Again."

The line went dead. I set the phone in its cradle, still laughing, and went into the bathroom. In the mirror, my face looked old and shapeless. I punched the wall, surprised by how easily my fist broke through the plaster. I turned off the light and climbed into the empty bathtub, soothed by the close walls, the low drone of the ceiling fan. I draped towels over the tub to make a roof for myself. I'd stopped laughing. I'd stopped crying. Minutes passed. Hours. Days, maybe. I experienced each moment of emptiness, the building unusually quiet, as if had been evacuated for an impending natural disaster. I slept and woke and slept again. Hunger gnawed at me, then left me alone. Eventually, a thin voice came to me through the darkness, a voice I recognized as my father's, eroded to a low, barely audible pitch, as if he were speaking through an impossibly long tube. I slipped into that tube, shimmying back several years to a grey blurred street. A January drizzle. A cold phone against my ear.

"Dad?"

"Felix." Dad sounded tired. "How are you?"

"I'm all right," I said. "I'm good."

I took a drag on my cigarette and looked up and down the street to see if anyone had followed me, if anyone was watching.

"Are you on a payphone?" he asked.

"Yeah. Thanks for taking the charges."

"It's fine."

"I didn't want to call from the house. They're always listening."

"Okay," he said, his voice carefully neutral.

I hopped from foot to foot. My skin hurt from exposure to the outside world. "I would have called sooner," I said, speaking quickly. "But I've been really busy. I got a job at a warehouse. A part-time thing. And I've started writing this book."

"I see." He didn't ask me to elaborate. A silence descended on the line.

"How's Eileen?" I asked.

"Your sister's fine. She's in Australia now."

"Right, I knew that. Did I know that?"

"I'm sure I mentioned it. She's been travelling for months now."

"Huh."

More silence. My body ached to get moving. "So you're working," Dad said, not a question, but a statement.

"Yeah."

"That's good."

"Actually..." I rubbed the side of my head. "The part-time thing didn't work out. I've got some leads, though."

Dad didn't answer. I pictured him in a pair of ironed blue jeans and a plain white T-shirt, tethered to the wall by our old rotary phone, snow in the window, faded flowers on the walls. Tears filled my eyes. I fought the urge to slam the receiver against the side of my head. "Well," I said. "I just wanted to check in."

"How are you doing for money?"

I flexed my jaw and dropped my damp cigarette on the pavement. "Now that you mention it...rent's coming up soon."

"I see."

"I don't need much." I crushed the cigarette under my foot, obliterating it.

"I understand," Dad said.

"A couple of hundred should get me through."

"I'll put something in your account tomorrow."

"You don't have to."

"I realize that."

"All right. Thanks."

I sagged in shame, the transaction over. There was nothing left to say. I missed Dad the instant I hung up, but knew that if I'd gotten him back on the line, I'd have only wanted to hang up all over again. Strangers passed, probing me with their eyes. I pulled up my hood and walked down the street, trying not to think about how my roommates had been going through my things, stealing my food, filling my head with subliminal messages while I was sleeping. The world tipped down and I stumbled over my own feet. Hardly knowing how I'd gotten there, I found myself at the bottom of a steep set of stairs on a rocky shoreline. Empty mansions loomed on a cliff behind me. The sea looked stagnant and dull. I sat down on a driftwood log and peered through the rain at a distant container ship, unable to tell what direction it was going, or if in fact it was moving at all. It seemed to me that the ship had always been there, always would be there, just as those same gulls would always be stamped against the sky on ragged, crucified wings. I hated the dull coastal winters with their endless drizzle. I wanted to go home, to the snowy fields and the wide-open skies of the prairies. But for all Dad's efforts to keep me off the streets, he'd seemed happy to leave me right where I was ever since I'd dropped out of school, making it known in countless small ways that home didn't want me back.

» » »

I put off calling Dad, specifically because Eileen had suggested it. If there was one thing I didn't need, it was more bad news. I assumed that he would pick up the phone if it was important enough, although I couldn't remember a single instance of him calling me in the past. When I thought about it, it seemed that our estrangement was directly connected to Mathilda's death, an event I'd revisited more than once since Eileen's phone call. One afternoon when I was in my early teens, I'd stumbled on Dad's stash of girlie magazines in the garden shed and put them to immediate use. After I'd stowed everything away, I stepped out into the backyard and Mathilda rushed me without warning, crossing the yard low and fast. I watched her come, thinking she wanted to play. I just had time to raise a defensive arm before she hit me, pinning me back against the shed. I shouted, in surprise more than anything, waiting for her to recognize me and let go, but she held on tight, her teeth tearing through my sleeve to anchor in the flesh of my arm.

I screamed for help, no longer knowing where I was, or what was happening, jostled from the shame-filled aftermath of furtive self-pleasure into what felt like a panicked struggle for my life. Mathilda leaned on her haunches and shook her head. I pulled back, bellowing in terror. Then, the door to the house flew open and Dad came thundering down the porch.

"Mathilda!"

She let go instantly and loped over to him with her tail flagging, as if abandoning a friendly game of tug-of-war.

"What the hell happened?" Dad shouted. "What did you do to her?"

"Nothing," I said, shocked.

He strode across the lawn, then stopped, going pale. "You're bleeding."

On the way to the vet clinic, I kept my wounded arm in an improvised bandage, while Mathilda sat tied up in the back, gazing out the window with interest. The veterinarian, an older man who looked like he'd have been more comfortable handling livestock than family pets, examined her briefly, then sighed and pushed his glasses up on his forehead. "Well, she isn't rabid," he said. "It could be some other neurological problem, but really, that's just guesswork. You say the attack was completely random? Nothing led up to it?"

Dad looked at me.

"What?" I said. "I didn't touch her!"

Dad sighed.

"Has she ever bitten anyone before?" the vet asked. "Or threatened to bite?"

"Absolutely not," Dad said.

"Hm." The vet frowned at Mathilda like a mechanic at a failing automobile. "I'd almost feel better if she had."

"How do you know if it's neurological?" Dad asked.

"Honestly? You don't. I mean there are tests, but I don't have the resources you need and you'd be looking at quite the expense. At the end of the day, the results wouldn't be a hundred percent conclusive anyway." It was hot in the clinic and Mathilda had started to pant. I hung back in a corner of the room, my arm hardly hurting anymore.

"So?" Dad said, leaving the obvious question unspoken.

"She's a big dog," the vet said, carefully. "An older dog."

Mathilda kept sitting nicely, letting the humans talk, not knowing how dire her situation had just become.

Dad turned to me. "Are you *sure* that you didn't provoke her?"

I nodded. Unless some glitch in her brain, or in the fabric of time itself, had caused her to skip back to the day when I'd thrown her against the wall as a puppy, I hadn't done a thing.

On the drive home, Dad didn't say a word. I sat in the back, where Mathilda had been not long before, remembering how she'd looked when we left her, how she'd stood up, expecting to follow us, but had found herself bound to the veterinarian's hand. I tried to imagine an alternate future for her, some shred of hope: the vet leading her out the back door of the clinic to an idling truck, the truck taking her out of the city to a sprawling acreage, where a group of friendly dogs would race to greet her. It wasn't impossible. If some people were secretly cruel to animals, couldn't others be secretly kind?

Outside the house, Dad killed the engine and pinned me in the rear-view mirror with his eyes. "What were you doing in the shed?"

My face went hot. "What do you mean?"

"You said you'd come out of the shed when it happened. What were you doing in the shed?"

"I...I don't know."

"You don't know."

I shook my head, trying very hard not to cry. Eileen stepped out onto the porch, arms folded, features pinched—a soldier's wife, anticipating the worst.

Dad stared at me for a long time, his face devoid of sympathy or love. Then he looked at his watch and sighed. "Well, she'll be in the freezer by now." He got out and walked slowly towards the house, leaving me alone in the back seat of the car.

» » »

The alley behind the Chinese grocer was dark, the nearest streetlight burnt out. As I peered up at the lit window on the second floor, I felt like I'd stepped into a magical pocket of private space, like a peep show booth, or a dim confessional. If Kim had come to the window and looked straight down, she wouldn't have seen me. But it wasn't Kim that I wanted to see, it was Jasmine. I assumed she was up there, listening to one of Kim's endless stories, a bottle of tequila on the table between them, something folksy on the stereo.

It had taken me weeks to find them. The night I threw the phone, Kim's number jostled off redial, erasing my last connection to her. Ever since, I'd been lingering around her favourite haunts: the thrift store, the library, the seawall. I spent entire days in the dog park, scrutinizing every curly-haired woman I saw. It was by chance alone that I eventually saw both Kim and Jasmine sharing a joint on a fire escape behind the Chinese grocer—a vague, half-second glimpse from the window of a passing bus, sharpening in retrospect like a Polaroid photograph. By the time I got off and doubled back, they were gone, but I'd marked the window they'd been standing by. After our last conversation, the desperate affection I'd felt for Kim had morphed into unadulterated hatred. I hated her for forcing her way into my life. I hated her for leaving. I hated her for stealing Jasmine just when she'd finally come back. Something about the way they'd embraced at the university left no doubt that they'd been more than friends. Down in the alley, I felt like I had a video feed from their apartment wired directly to my brain. I saw Kim put her hand over Jasmine's, claiming her. I watched her place a single pink pill on Jasmine's tongue. Then Jasmine got up and began to dance—swaying lazily, while Kim sat back with her knees apart, a faint smile playing around her mouth. I groped at my feet and jerked my hand back as a broken bottle sliced my thumb. Sucking at the cut, I reached with my other hand and found what I was looking for: a decent-sized rock. A shadow passed across the window above me, a subtle change in light. With my thumb still in my mouth, I fixed a bead on the window and threw. The rock bounced off the wall and fell to the pavement with a soft clatter. No one came to the window. No one told me to stop. I felt at my feet again, pushing aside old plastic containers and scraps of cardboard, until I'd uncovered a broken chunk of concrete, heavy as a fossilized egg. I turned it over in my hands, feeling it had been deposited there years ago by an invisible accomplice. The concrete fit the grooves of my throwing hand perfectly. I turned my face up to the luminescent rectangle of the window, plotting the concrete's trajectory from hand to glass and beyond—through the apartment, past Jasmine, into the side of Kim's head. And at that instant, with that image in my mind, I threw with everything that I had.

CHAPTER SEVEN

Somewhere outside, car doors slammed. Indistinct voices resounded in the parking lot. I approached the curtains warily, as if they'd been draped over the cage of a wild animal. An unfamiliar car was parked directly below my window. The sky hung low and dark, the streetlights glowing softly. Across the way, the pale man sat in a chair, staring at nothing. A polite rapping came at my door and I tensed, then immediately relaxed, assuming police had finally come. My aim at the Chinese's grocer had been true. Kim's window hadn't shattered, but I'd damaged the glass and now I would have to pay. Not just for the window, but for my intent. A charge of attempted murder would not have been unjustified. After weeks of dread, I was almost looking forward to my confession. But when I opened the door, I found the building superintendent, looking as surprised to see me as I was to see her.

"Oh," she said. "You *are* home."

"Yes," I said, unsettled by the way my voice hung in the air. A fruit fly landed on my arm and I brushed it away. The superintendent tried to peer around me into the apartment and I widened my shoulders to block her view.

"I just wanted to make sure that you were aware of the laundry situation," she said.

"Sorry, what situation?"

"The washing machines. They're out of order."

"Oh?" The floor shifted under my feet.

"Thieves," she said bitterly. "Broke them right open. The repairman should be in later this week. In the meantime, I've been telling people to use the laundromat down the block."

I nodded, thinking she looked thinner, with dark pouches under her eyes. "Okay."

"It's hard to believe what some people will do for a handful of quarters, don't you think?"

A soft rustling came from the apartment behind me and I looked over my shoulder. When I turned back, the superintendent was watching me closely.

"Was there something else?" I asked.

"Well, now that you mention it, there was one other thing. Mr. Colombo—he lives next to you, you know. He mentioned that he's been hearing noises from your apartment."

"Oh?" I glanced down the hall at his unit, feeling him on the on the other side of his door, listening.

"He said he heard the sound of, well…someone being emotional."

"I see."

"Apparently, it's been disturbing his sleep. Now, I don't mean to pry, but I was wondering if you're—"

"I'm fine," I said, more sharply than I'd intended.

"Well. If you need anything…"

"I appreciate that."

"All right. Have a good night, Mr. Mallory."

I shut the door and fruit flies swirled around me, then settled on the walls. I wondered how they perceived me, if they recognized me as a fellow creature, or if I was just some colossal force of nature to them. I leaned in close to an individual and stared at its tiny red eyes. I let it feel my breath on its wings. When it didn't move, I slowly raised one hand and extended my index finger. I paused with the tip of my finger millimetres away from its delicate exoskeleton. Then I lowered my hand

and looked around, overwhelmed by the thought of returning my apartment to a state of livability.

The old man next door was watching an action movie, the bass vibrating through the wall. I grabbed a bottle of wine from the counter and took a long slug. Warm fingers pushed up my spine. I carried the bottle into the bedroom and stopped. A large pile of change shone on the nightstand. No pennies, no nickels or dimes. Only quarters. I stared at the money, then turned off the light and eased into bed, listening to the staccato pulse of machine-gun fire next door. Eventually, the old man's television went quiet. I watched the interplay of light and shadows on my ceiling, unable to sleep. Kim had lost the power to hurt me, the hurled rock having broken whatever spell I'd been under, but Jasmine still tumbled around in my head. As I began to drift off, a faint, whispery sound came from out in the living area. I held my breath, hearing it again, a match rasping against a strip of phosphorous. I went out to investigate and the sound intensified, growing urgent. Something was trapped in the cupboard under the sink, scrabbling and banging about. The longer I stared at the door, the louder the noise became. With my heart thudding in my ears, I gripped the handle and pulled. The garbage can under the sink had been knocked over, rotten food and scraps of plastic everywhere. In the middle of the pile, not looking the least bit afraid, sat a large grey rat. It glared at me defiantly, like an old man who'd been disturbed on the toilet. "Sorry," I said. The rat watched me for a moment, then seemed to decide I wasn't a threat and shuffled off to one side, as if inviting me to join it in the cupboard.

"No," I said. "That's all right."

The rat gave the rat equivalent of a shrug and returned to its feast. I shut the cupboard door and fell back into bed.

» » »

I woke to the sound of the building collapsing around me. The windows bucked and shuddered. Outside, giant apes were pounding on the hoods of cars, flipping over garbage bins, scaling the walls of my building and heaving at the framework. Coming fully awake, I recognized the storm for what it was. Hurricanes didn't generally happen on that side of the continent, but gale force winds occasionally roared in from the sea to batter my windows and fling debris around the parking lot. The appliances were dark, the power out. I pushed to my feet and headed for the balcony door. The entire neighbourhood had gone black. Bright shards of insanity flashed through my head. A spray of coins across linoleum. The superintendent on her hands and knees, naked from the waist down. An ancient hand reaching out of a heating vent. A hard gust hit the building and the sliding door bowed inwards. I pictured it exploding, blowing glass into my face, my eyes. I stayed where I was, willing it to happen, wanting to be sucked into the night like a stack of paper blown from the window of a speeding car. The glass unflexed. Feeling compelled to be out in the thick of the storm, I threw on my jacket and stepped out into the pitch-black hall. The walls sighed as I felt my way past the old man's unit and down the stairs to the main level. I shoved at the back door and the wind pushed back. On my second try, the wind ripped the door from my hands and threw it against the side of the building. I staggered out into the parking lot, dodging plastic bags and billowing sheets of newspaper. The sky was bright orange, the road littered with branches. Looking up, I saw the pale man at his window with a lit candle. He raised one hand and I headed for the road. I clambered over an uprooted tree and jogged past a streetlight fluttering on a wire like a paper clip on a string. The wind filled my head, my jacket ballooning behind me as I made my way through the empty streets, heading downhill, towards the ocean. Whitecaps flared in the distance. But as I approached the road that hugged the coastline, terror jolted me to a standstill. The ocean had breached the seawall. A line of darkness surged over the road and stopped just short of the spot where I was standing, then drew back and slipped out of sight. Beside me, a flag banged at the top of a pole. I felt like a sleepwalker, woken to find myself in true mortal danger. A red truck glided past me on the street, the driver oddly familiar. I thought about waving him off, but he approached the T-junction at the end of the road so confidently that I assumed he knew what he was doing. The moment he made the turn, another wave flooded the road. The water couldn't have been that deep, but the back end of the truck started to drift. I could see the driver fighting with the wheel. The sea retracted, hauling in its catch. The truck spun in slow motion. For a moment, I could hear the faint drone of a car horn over the roaring wind. Then the truck reached the edge of the seawall and went over.

Waves advanced a third time, the trees along the road all bending in the same direction, away from the sea. I tore my eyes from the spot where the truck had disappeared and sprinted up the slope, letting the wind carry me past darkened houses and storefronts, over the fallen tree and back to my building, where the remains of a heavy clay pot were strewn about the parking lot. A chained garbage bin kept arrhythmic time to the storm. The pale man's window had gone dark. I felt my way up the stairwell and down the hall to my unit, where I locked my door, picked up the phone, and dialed 911. A bored operator came on the line. I gave her a rough outline of what I'd just seen and she repeated the story back to me in a skeptical monotone.

"Yes, that's right," I said.

"You saw a truck drive off the seawall at the intersection of Coast and Bank."

"It didn't drive off. It was pulled off."

"Pulled off."

"That's right. By the waves."

"I'm not following you."

"From the storm," I said, impatiently.

The operator went quiet. "When did you say this happened, sir?"

"I don't know. About twenty minutes ago. I can't say exactly. My power's been—"

I broke off. The power had been restored. The lights might have been off, but my appliances were all humming, and the clock on the stove read two in the morning. I couldn't hear the wind anymore. In fact, the apartment couldn't have been quieter.

"Sir," the operator said. "Would you mind going over this one more time with me?"

I carried the phone to the window and pulled back the curtains. The parking lot was well lit and still as a museum display. The strewn garbage was gone. The tree I'd clambered over to get to the road was standing where it had always stood.

"Sir?" the voice said in my ear.

"I'm sorry," I said. "I made a mistake."

"A mistake," she repeated

"I fell asleep on the couch. I was confused. I must have been dreaming."

"Dreaming."

"That's right."

"Sir," she said after a long pause. "Would you like me to connect you with our mental health department?"

"No, no," I said. "I'm just…I'm sorry for disturbing you."

The operator was reluctant to let me go, asking if I'd been doing any drugs, if I was under a psychiatrist's care. I repeatedly assured her that I was fine and hung up, still standing at the window, staring at the magically restored tree. My face was raw from the wind, my ears ringing. Eventually, I became aware of the answering machine blinking on a side table. I had messages waiting, twelve of them, the most the machine could hold. I turned on the overhead light, momentarily stunned by the state of the apartment. It looked like it had been ransacked, with hardly a square inch of floor space to walk through, the walls smeared with grime, clouds of fruit flies swarming all around me. I sat down amid the filth to listen to the messages, starting with the most recent. A tinny version of my sister's voice filled the room.

"Just got back from the service. It was nice, I guess. Still waiting for you to call. Seriously, Felix. This is getting ridiculous."

A flutter of dread went through me at the word "service." I skipped to the preceding message.

"Leaving for the funeral home now. I don't know if you've been getting these messages, but I hope you're going to be there. I really don't want to have to do this alone...."

On the next message, Eileen confirmed what I'd already suspected. Dad was gone. I listened to message after message, all from my sister, hearing her grief unfold in reverse order, from acceptance to denial, and back further, to the anticipation of grief, when she'd first learned how serious his diagnosis was, how little time he had left. Finally, only one message remained. I pushed the play button, expecting to hear my sister's voice again. Instead, after a few seconds of dead air, I heard my father, sounding weak and defeated, his voice barely louder than a whisper. "Felix—"

I stopped the machine. Until that moment, I'd felt strangely detached, as if learning about the death of a minor character in a novel, an event that had been foreshadowed and brought to fruition at exactly the right moment. But the sound of Dad's voice touched something dangerous inside of me, something I wasn't sure I could survive.

A sudden, insistent scratching came at the kitchen cupboard. The rat was awake. I'd been feeding it for weeks, out of fear, throwing table scraps directly into the cupboard under the sink and quickly shutting the door, not wanting to see the animal, imagining it must have doubled or tripled in size. I threw a shoe at the cupboard and the scratching stopped. I began to erase the messages, pushing the delete button savagely, the evidence against me shrinking with each jab of the finger. When I came to the last message, I hesitated, then pushed the button one more time, erasing Dad's final words to me before I'd even heard them. Then, just as methodically, with the same button-pressing motion of my index finger, I went around the apartment crushing every fruit fly I could find, climbing onto furniture to get at the ones on the ceiling. A few tried to escape, but for the most part they seemed to have no instinct for self-preservation, passively awaiting their destruction. By the time the sun rose, I'd killed more than I could count. Not daring to rest, I gathered the surface clutter into garbage bags, hauled my dirty clothes to the basement, and crammed them into the newly repaired machines, using the quarters from my nightstand. That done, I stalked down to the corner store and purchased some cleaning supplies and a large rat trap.

Back home, I attacked the walls and floors with a stiff brush. I disinfected the bathroom, dusted the furniture, and finished the laundry. I organized everything I hadn't thrown out and fashioned traps for the remaining fruit flies out of funnels of paper and baited glasses. Finally, I unwrapped the rat trap and carried it into the kitchen. I braced myself before opening the cupboard, half-expecting the rat to launch itself at me, but found only savaged food containers and piles of little brown turds. I swept it all out, put the trap down, smeared the catch with peanut butter and slammed the cupboard door. The sun was coming through the window at a low angle, painting everything gold. An entire day had gone by. Too tired to put sheets on the bed, I collapsed on the bare mattress, the events of the past twenty-four hours settling around me—the revelation on the machine, the imagined storm—and as I returned to the face of the man in the truck, I realized who it was he'd reminded me of. He'd looked exactly like my father.

I opened my eyes and found Dad frowning down at me—not a mental projection of the person he used to be, but his actual self, occupying physical space. I smelled his sour breath, felt his hand on my arm.

"Dad?"

"You okay?" he asked.

I tried to sit up, and he eased me back down.

"It's all right. You were just having a nightmare."

"I was?"

"Sounded that way."

I lay back and he smoothed down my hair, an unusually tender gesture. "Big week coming up. New teacher. New grade. It's normal to be nervous."

"No," I said. "It wasn't about school. It was…" I looked at Dad, a hot pain stabbing my chest. "Something happened to you. I dreamed you'd died."

"Oh yeah?" He laughed. "Do I look dead to you?"

I shook my head. But the truth was, he didn't look quite alive either.

"It was just a dream," he said.

I nodded. "Okay."

Mathilda came into the room, wagging her tail as she padded over to the bed.

My clown nightlight cast a weak glow from one corner of the room. Dad's eyes were heavy, like he'd been drinking. I wondered if he'd been looking at his magazines again—catalogues, I assumed, of ladies he was thinking about marrying (although I couldn't have said why they weren't wearing any clothes, or why the poses they struck made me feel like going to the bathroom). He adjusted my covers, then stood back, his face in shadow.

"So what happened to me?" he asked. "In your dream?"

"I'm not sure," I mumbled.

"Come on," he said, with what felt like forced levity. "You must remember something. You said I'd died. How did it happen? How did I die?"

In the dim room, he looked very old. I struggled to keep my eyes open, blearily gazing at the clown light. "You were…" The dream was fading, but I still had a hold on it. I could almost see it, shimmering under the surface of my consciousness. But before I could pull it out, the dream pulled back, dragging me down with it into darkness.

CHAPTER EIGHT

Once I'd set the apartment in order, the chaos of my life settled. The natural rhythms of the building returned. The clock made sense. I still thought about Jasmine and Kim, but my father's death had put the situation firmly into perspective. A few days after hearing my sister's messages, I phoned her in New Zealand, claiming to have been away, and she completed the picture for me, explaining how Dad had kept his diagnosis to himself until the last week of his life, how the cancer moved more quickly than even the doctors had expected, as if he'd made the conscious decision not to fight. She'd flown home to be with him at the end and said that he'd been heavily drugged, swimming through different periods of his life, speaking to her as if she were people he'd known in the past—a teacher, his mother, his wife.

"Did he talk about me?" I asked.

She hesitated. "Well... no. But he wasn't exactly himself. Anyway, we need to talk about his estate. There wasn't much. A bit of savings and the house. Dad wanted us to split everything evenly between us.

"So I own half a house?"

"I thought we could rent it out," Eileen said. "Until we decide what to do with it. I know someone in town who can deal with the tenants. You'll get a monthly cheque. You won't have to do a thing."

The idea of anyone other than Dad living in the house felt strange, but it was a twenty-hour drive from my apartment, and I could think of nothing better to do with it. I hung up, feeling both relieved and ashamed to have gotten off so easily. I was deep in debt. The inheritance couldn't have come at a better time, as if my father's death had been brought about for the sole purpose of rescuing me financially. I tried to summon tears, but we'd been apart for so long that I could barely remember what he'd looked like. What memories I had were unclear, distorted by the dread I'd always felt in his presence, not of what he might do, but of what he might be thinking, his features eclipsed by the insurmountable force of his disappointment in me.

My sister was able to forward me part of the inheritance, and I paid my overdue bills and reconnected to the internet, navigating to my email account, where I found messages from my agent and publisher, but nothing from Kim. I thought about having a drink, and gently pushed the craving away. The secret to quitting, I'd found, lay in taking pleasure from deprivation. I punished myself with three sets of push-ups and crunches, then lay exhausted on the floor, looking over at my bookshelf. I couldn't remember the last time I'd actually read a book. I went over and ran my hand along the spines, feeling the old flicker of anticipation, the almost pornographic allure of climbing into another person's head. I shut my eyes and selected a book at random, carrying it over to the sofa without looking at it, wanting to experience the first page without preconceptions. But the moment I sat down, a distinct noise came from the kitchen, the whisper of fur against wood. I looked back at the cupboard under the sink. The fruit flies might have gone, but the rat was still with me. I'd been checking the trap multiple times a day, seeing nothing but the locked garbage can, a bottle of bleach, and the turds the rat left behind, as if to mock me, or punish me, for depriving it of its steady diet of trash. Every time I swept out its droppings, rage would spike through my head and I would picture myself destroying the animal in outlandishly violent ways—taking a knife to it, a hammer, a bat. Crouched in front of the open cupboard, I would shine a light into its ragged hole and threaten it through clenched teeth, daring it to come out and face me.

The rustling stopped. The instant I returned my attention to the book in my hand, it started up again, louder than before, as if the rat were not only watching, but deliberately taunting me. I stared at the silent cupboard for a full minute, then threw my book aside, strode into the kitchen, and tore open the door. I slammed the bottle of bleach in front of the hole and returned to my spot on the sofa. Before I'd read two words, the sound returned, more of a gnawing than a rustling this time. I went back and thumped around under the sink, thinking the noise would scare the rat away for a little while at least, but the gnawing started up again the moment I shut the door. I jabbed a fork down into the hole, splashed bleach all around it. If I'd had something explosive, I would have shoved it in without hesitation. For the better part of an hour, I sat cross-legged in front of the open cupboard, my book forgotten.

"Come out," I commanded. "Come out!"

But the rat had finally gone away. Across the room, my laptop beckoned—an open portal to distraction. I went over and googled myself, finding a smattering of reviews of *The Pole*, most of them damningly ambivalent. I opened a new page and searched for adult webcams, my self-control unravelling. A pop-up ad for a dating site obscured the search results. I started to click it away, then paused, knowing enough about the internet to know that these advertisements were tailored to my specific needs and desires. They were trying to sell me something they thought I might use. I touched the link and a stylized pink and blue yin-yang filled my screen. After I'd entered some basic personal information—age, location, credit card—the site invited me to browse through profiles of female members.

Of the several dozen women in my area, only five were online, none of whom had profile photos. The youngest, Miss Bliss (Female, 19), sent me a cluttered shorthand of numbers, letters, and symbols, suggesting we meet that very night. A low buzz of fear ran up the back of my head. I ignored the message, sending tentative hellos to the other four women, but received no reply. I was just about to log out and return to my hunt for Jasmine when a new user came online, going by the name Twice Shy (Female, 28). Seven years younger than me. Unlike the other active users, Twice Shy did have a profile photo, not of herself but of a majestic white unicorn head. The photo gave me pause, but I sent her a message anyway, ignoring the notes from Miss Bliss piling up in my inbox. After a minute, a notification appeared on my screen:

Twice Shy wants to chat with you now!

I knew that I would be charged for activating the live chat feature, but I also knew that if I failed to accept the invitation, I would spend the rest of the night wondering if I'd done the right thing. The exchange would be completely anonymous. The fee wasn't that high. I pushed the green accept button and a chat room opened, where Twice Shy appeared to be waiting.

Hello, she typed.

Hi, I wrote back.

Her cursor blinked, before the next message came. *How are you?*

Not bad. I slid my free hand down the waistband of my pants. *Yourself?*

I've been better.

My hand stopped. This was going in a different direction than I'd hoped.

What's wrong? I asked, out of politeness more than anything.

People suck.

I nodded at my screen. *Yes,* I agreed. *They do.*

Why is that? Twice Shy asked. *Why are people so horrible?*

That's a good question.
I've decided to give up on them. I've taken a strict vow of solitude.
You do realize you're on a dating site.
Online doesn't count. Besides, I'm only here for the penis pics.
I laughed out loud, then typed *lol* for her benefit.
I'm serious, she wrote back. *I've been collecting them for years. I only take the unsolicited ones. I have nearly five hundred so far.*
Wow. Um... why do you do this?
It's an art project. I print them out on my printer.
Really?
Really. I've filled nearly a whole album. And not a small one either. One of those great big wedding albums.
Do you show this book to company?
I never have company, remember?
Right. I inched my free hand towards my waistband again, uncertain how to take all this penis talk.
I'm surprised you haven't sent me one already, she wrote.
I was thinking about it, I joked.
Were you?
No!
It's nothing to be ashamed of. It seems like the standard greeting these days.
You're telling me you wouldn't find it strange.
Not at all.
That's bizarre.
Actually, it's perfectly normal for male primates to display their genitals in certain social situations. One might argue that it's abnormal to conceal them.
Interesting perspective.
Are you very lonely? she asked.
I looked up from the screen, startled by the abrupt shift in direction.
Yes, I admitted.
Do you want to talk about it?

At this point, I committed to the keyboard with both hands, opening up about everything I'd been going through, from the breakup with Kim to my father's death to the rat that lived under my sink. I told Twice Shy about my paranoia, my isolation, my blocks of missing time, and she sounded genuinely interested. More than that, she sounded like she understood. When I started talking about time travel, she wrote, *We should get married.*

I could feel myself smiling foolishly.

Or at least go for coffee? I ventured, my heart beating a little faster.

Where do you live? she asked.

Close to downtown.

What?

I hesitated, then typed: *Bank.*

A long pause came on her end. *What direction does your window face?*

My body went rigid. Up to this point, it had been a harmless game. I hadn't intended to reveal my true identity to her or anyone else. She had no idea what I looked like, what I did for a living. I still had time to sever the connection, to stop whatever was about to happen. I half-shut my laptop, then opened it again and typed: *South.*

After another long silence, she wrote, *Go to your window.*

I peered through a crack in the curtains at the low-rise across the way, not seeing anything unusual. Then, beyond the low-rise, in one of the taller buildings in the distance I saw a square of light going on and off repeatedly

When I got back to the laptop, I saw that she'd written, *Do you see me?*

The cursor blinked, awaiting my reply. *Yes.*

I have coffee.

I made it down to the lobby without running into anyone. Outside, the street was quiet, the sky an unusual shade of yellow, a fine mist dampening my face and clothes. The light blinked in the sky at regular intervals, like a beacon on a lighthouse. I walked towards it, zigzagging through the streets, occasionally losing sight of the building, but always finding it again. Two blocks away, I stopped and counted windows, then counted again, concluding that her unit was on the west corner of the sixteenth floor. I crossed the street to avoid the grub-like form of a person cocooned around a heat grate. A man appeared behind me, weaving down the sidewalk. I had the feeling that these elements were being strategically dropped into place, forcing me towards the increasingly ominous face of Twice Shy's apartment building. The front door was propped open with a battered tennis shoe. I intended to walk right past, but a second, glowering man stepped out of an alley in front of me. I ducked through the apartment entrance, passing under dim fluorescents to a pair of elevator doors, one of which appeared to be permanently out of service. The glowering man followed me into the building. I frantically pushed the up button, wishing I'd thought to remove the tennis shoe. The elevator door jerked open and I leaped inside, noting the distinct odors of piss and old vomit. The man lurched across lobby, staring at me with red-rimmed eyes. I jabbed at the number sixteen, and the door slid shut on him.

As the elevator shuddered up to the sixteenth floor, I exhaled and leaned back against the car's fake wood paneling. The digital display above the door was broken, leaving some doubt as to just what floor I'd come to when the doors finally opened. I stepped into the empty hall, feeling that I'd entered the body of a huge sleeping animal. The walls were the colour of uncooked liver, the carpet a muddy brown. I tried to orient myself, heading uncertainly down the hall in what seemed like a westerly direction. A couple was arguing loudly behind one door, a television blaring porn behind another. The door at the end of the hall was open half an inch. I had no idea what lay behind it. I pictured a hulking man with duct tape, zip-ties, and a hunting knife. Obeying an almost suicidal impulse, I gently nudged the door open. Nothing. The interior of the apartment looked shabby but tidy, an empty living space illuminated by a shaded table lamp. I crossed the threshold, smelling freshly brewed coffee. A floorboard groaned under my weight.

A chuffing noise came from the back room.

"Quiet!" a woman hissed. Then louder, to me: "Is that you?"

"Yes," I croaked back.

"We're in here."

We?

I closed the door behind me and followed the voice to a brightly lit kitchen, where a woman in sunglasses was standing beside a large yellow dog. The woman's long dark hair was brushed forward to conceal much of her face. Her baggy clothes looked like they'd come off a men's rack. The dog barked once and she made a sharp noise to quiet it. "This is Boris," she said. "He's harmless."

"Okay," I said, not moving.

"I didn't think you'd come."

"Neither did I," I admitted.

"I made coffee." She pointed at the machine on the counter. "Just in case."

"Okay." I still didn't move, wondering if she could see me.

"I'm not blind," she said, guessing what I'd been thinking. "I just prefer the dark."

"I see."

"So do I," she said, then shook her head. "Sorry, that was corny." She fussed with something on the counter. Even with half her face obscured I could see she was blushing. "Do you still want coffee?"

"That would be nice," I said, disarmed by her awkwardness.

The dog came over to sniff my crotch as the woman filled two cups and carried them through a second door out to the living room, the apartment having a circular layout. We sat on opposite ends of a small loveseat and Boris settled at our feet. In front of us, a framed poster of a white unicorn hung on the wall—a muscular animal rearing up on its hind legs, steam jetting from its nostrils.

"I'm Zoe, by the way."

"Felix."

"Cool."

In the silence that followed, I could hear both the argument and the faint sound of porn continuing down the hall. The computer the woman must have been writing on glowed through her open bedroom door.

"Sorry," I finally said. "I'm not much of a conversationalist."

She ran her fingers through her hair. "That's okay. Neither am I."

The unicorn in the poster looked unsettlingly realistic. I wondered if they'd attached a prosthetic horn to a horse, or added the detail digitally after the fact. "So ..." Zoe said after a minute. "Do you want to see my art project?"

"Sure," I said, wondering if it would involve unicorns.

"Okay. Give me a second." She went into the bedroom and emerged with a large photo album. I opened the front cover and felt my face get very warm. I thought she'd been joking about the penis pictures, but here they were, six different cocks on every page of one very thick book. With Zoe looking over my shoulder, I experienced a confused rush of embarrassment and sexual excitement. I started to laugh, but she remained perfectly serious. I cleared my throat and turned the page. The photos were obviously self-portraits, some showing a man's entire naked body in a mirror, most confined to the genitals.

"Hmm," I said, thoughtfully. My initial excitement faded as I turned the page, confronted by organs of every size and colour, some circumcised, some not, some flaccid, some erect. Not one stood out as being remarkable in any way. I might as well have been looking at a catalogue of noses, or elbows. I turned another page.

"I try to make sure that there's no doubles," Zoe said. "To keep it fair."

"How do you mean?"

"Well..." She frowned to herself. "Having a hundred pictures of the same man would defeat the whole purpose. It isn't a turn-on for me. The way I see it, I'm doing these men a kindness. They want someone to look at them. So I look."

I kept turning pages, feeling increasingly ashamed, as if I'd taken every one of those pictures myself. When I came to the end, I sat with the book in my lap.

"Do you think I'm strange?" she asked, timidly.

"No."

"Really?"

I tried to find her eyes behind the dark lenses. "I'm pretty strange myself."

"Like with the time travelling?"

"For starters."

"Where do you go?" she asked, intrigued.

"To the past, mostly." It felt odd, discussing it so frankly. "But every once in a while I see things that haven't happened yet."

"The future."

"More like a possible future. I don't know. Maybe I'm just crazy."

"I don't think you're crazy," she said decisively. Although we hardly knew each other, I found her confidence reassuring. "Did you see all this before it happened?" she asked. "Coming here? Meeting me?"

"I don't know. Maybe."

"So...what happens next?"

Still holding the penis album, I looked at Zoe, seeing my own face reflected in her dark lenses. I shook my head. "I'm not really sure."

CHAPTER NINE

The chestnut trees lining the sidewalk gave almost no shade. The humidity added ten pounds to my clothes. I wasn't sure where I was going but felt that it must have had something to do with Zoe. We'd been seeing each other for weeks. Whenever I felt lonely or out of sorts, I'd stop by her place, and feel instantly at ease, consoled by the sight of her eccentric sunglasses and unkempt hair. She'd put on coffee and we'd commiserate about the awfulness of our lives before moving to her bedroom and having urgent sex. I never felt pressured to stay the night, or to visit more often. In fact, she seemed to have no expectations of me whatsoever, accepting my erratic arrivals and departures with perfect equanimity.

I came to an abrupt stop. If I'd been going to Zoe's place, I was heading in the wrong direction.

"*Excuse* me," a woman behind me said.

"Sorry," I muttered and kept moving.

The sidewalk was crammed with attractive young people, swinging their naked limbs confidently through space. Wearing long sleeves and jeans myself, I slogged downhill until I came to a pit in the earth, surrounded by an eight-foot-tall chain-link fence. On one side of the fence, half a dozen men in hard hats and orange vests lounged around smoking as a large backhoe tore up the ground. On the pedestrian side, my next-door neighbour, the old door slammer, stood watching them intently, his hands knotted in the wire. As I hurried past, I heard him mutter, "Kill it."

The ocean must have been close. I could smell salt and decay. The sun burned on the back of my neck. I wanted to shrug off my clothes and leave them heaped in a pile on the sidewalk. As the seawall came into sight, along with dozens of joggers, bikers, and rollerbladers, I stopped in the middle of Coast Road, not realizing where I was until a horn blared. I hurried the rest of the way across and a red pickup roared past, the exact make and model that I'd seen on the night of the storm. The driver looked similar. Even the intersection was identical. I looked out past the seawall, half-expecting to find a tidal wave rolling in, but the water remained calm, the sky clear. The truck parked at an angle on the road, and the driver—the living image of my father—got out with what looked like camera gear and walked off down a sloping path to the beach. Gravity and light. The air in my lungs. As I approached the truck, I saw a little film canister wedged between the windshield and the dash. The passenger window was open. No one was looking my way. I walked up to the truck like it belonged to me, alarm bells jangling in my head as I punctured the invisible membrane between public and private space and snatched the film off the dash. The maneuver took all of three seconds, but the world changed dramatically in those three seconds. No one shouted or confronted me, but people suddenly looked uneasy, as if sensing my transgression. Inanimate objects leaned towards me: buildings, street signs, vehicles. I jammed the film in my pocket, then jogged across the street and ducked down a side road, nearly falling more than once as I looked over my shoulder, expecting the red truck to come roaring around the corner, the driver leaning grimly into the wheel. After a few blocks, I forced myself to slow to a normal pace, taking the long way home, through a trendy neighbourhood filled with coffee shops, where I stopped and pulled out the stolen canister, confirming that it in fact held a roll of used film. As I snapped the canister shut, a harsh cry rang out, and a dark shape swooped down from a tree, passing inches from the top of my head. A crow, flapping over the treetops. It hurled itself back down at me and I ducked and kept walking. I tried to keep a casual pace, as if nothing unusual was happening, but the crow buzzed me again, and people on the surrounding patios were starting to take notice. On the fourth pass, the bird made contact, raking its claws across my scalp. Abandoning any pretext of calmness, I covered my head and ran, past rows of townhouses and character homes with pristine lawns. Whenever I paused to look up, a dark flurry battered my face and drove me on. People were staring now, accusingly, as if I'd antagonized the bird, and deserved to be attacked. I sprinted the last few blocks to my apartment and slammed through the front doors, spinning to face the crow, who'd landed on the welcome mat outside. "Go away!" I yelled through the glass door.

"Hello, Felix," an icy voice behind me said.

I turned to find the superintendent standing in the middle of the lobby.

"I'm sorry," I gasped. "This bird…"

"I got your note," she said, ignoring the crow altogether.

"Excuse me?"

"Your note. I have to say, it came as a bit of a surprise." Her hair was fuller than I remembered, her hairline unnaturally low and slightly askew. "No, not a surprise," she corrected herself. "A disappointment."

I looked at her more closely, noting that her eyebrows had been painted on and that she had no lashes at all. She hadn't even glanced at the crow parked outside the door. "Three years." She advanced on me slowly. "Three years you've been with us. You'd think after all that time we would have earned some loyalty."

I took a step back, having no idea what she was talking about.

"I don't think," she continued evenly, "that you understand

how lucky you were to find us. You'll never see a rent so reasonable. Not in this location. A ten-minute walk to downtown. A twenty-minute walk to the ocean. Free parking. Free hot water..." She kept coming until she'd backed me up against the wall. I could smell the illness radiating off her, her clothes hanging loose on her frame, her eyes shimmering with eerie light. "It's not that we'll have trouble replacing you," she assured me. "We won't. There's a long waiting list. Oh, you should see our waiting list...I just wish you'd had the courtesy to tell me to my face. I wish—" She broke off, seized by a sudden, violent coughing fit. I circled around her, just as I would have circled a rabid dog. Her wig fell off and lay at her feet in a little black heap. Her face was pale and shining.

"I'm sorry." I hovered at the door to the stairwell, unsure what I was apologizing for.

The words seemed to give her renewed strength and she straightened, looking ageless, almost beautiful, her scalp covered by a dark fuzz, her skin so pale she was nearly translucent. "Yes," she said. "You are."

I wrenched open the door and began to climb, hearing the hydraulic arm catch behind me, bringing the door to a slow, hissing close.

Pain stabbed at my right ear the moment I arrived in my apartment. I pressed my hand against the side of my head and looked around, sensing another presence, some activity that had recently, and abruptly, stopped. Everything in the kitchen and living area seemed to be in order. I moved to the bedroom and listened at the closed door. A faint scratching came from inside. I thought about the rat, wondering if it had grown tired of waiting to be fed and had come looking for me. I slowly opened the door and found the room lit by dozens of tea lights, Zoe lying on the bed like a pale starfish: blindfolded and naked, her arms and legs fastened to the bedframe with short lengths of rope. She lay so still that for a moment I wondered if she was alive at all. Then I noticed the slight rise and fall of her chest, and the tented note on the bedside table: *Happy Birthday*.

I wanted to untie her and throw a blanket over her, shocked that she'd thought this would please me. She hardly participated in sex at the best of times, lying perfectly still, always asking the same tentative question afterwards: *Was that okay?* I walked around the bed, wondering how she'd managed to tie herself so firmly. I held my open hand just above her navel. I didn't touch her, but slowly moved my hand up her torso, gliding above the skin to her small breasts and unusually long neck. A strange violence entered me as I cupped my hand around the base of her throat, a desire to apply pressure. She didn't move, allowing me to keep my hand there. I pulled back and she arched towards me.

I prepared myself and climbed on top of her, trembling with lust. I put both hands around her throat—the blindfold like some dark gathering force, pulling me into her head. I climaxed almost immediately, then let go, seeing red marks where my fingers had been moments before.

"Jesus," I said softly.

Zoe was breathing quickly, her eyes still obscured. I rolled off her and loosened the knots at her wrists and ankles.

"Did you like that?" she asked, taking off the blindfold.

I couldn't answer, or even look at her.

She slipped on her prescription sunglasses. "What is it?"

"Nothing."

"I'm sorry...I thought you'd like it."

"I did like it."

"Then why are you mad?"

"I'm not mad."

"You seem mad."

"Can we drop this, please?"

I sat on the edge of the bed and she fell silent, her expression unreadable behind the dark lenses. I hadn't liked what had happened. I'd been consumed by it, having tapped into something sadistic and cruel that made me doubt everything I'd ever believed about myself: that I was, at heart, a decent person. It was true that I hadn't hurt her. Nor had she seemed to mind. But this wasn't about her. It was about me. I stared at my hands, going over everything that had happened since I came to on the sidewalk, the way a wasp explores a piece of rotten meat. The truck, the crow, the superintendent. And now this.

"What are you thinking about?" Zoe asked.

I jumped, having forgotten she was there, then shook my head. "Nothing."

"Are you having second thoughts?"

"About what?"

"Moving in with me."

Was that what was happening? I couldn't imagine what life with Zoe would look like. As it was, she barely existed for me.

"No," I said. "I'm just...distracted. There was a crow on the way home. It kept coming after me..."

"It must have been protecting its nest."

"There were plenty of other people around. It had no problem with them."

"Maybe you looked particularly threatening."

"I don't think so. This was personal. It was trying to deliver a message."

"What kind of message?"

"I don't know...That I don't belong in the world. That I was put here by mistake."

Zoe didn't laugh or contradict me, instead frowning sympathetically. "I'm sorry."

It was a novel sensation, being understood. In many ways, talking to Zoe felt like talking to myself, which might have explained why I felt so ambivalent about moving in with her. I went over to the window to look for the crow. When I turned around, Zoe was still on the bed, tears sliding down her face. "Sorry." She took off her glasses and wiped the tears away, viciously. "I just wish we weren't both so damaged…"

I knew that I should have said something comforting, or gone over to embrace her, but felt physically incapable of doing anything of the kind.

She put her glasses back on, looking like she had something terrible to say. "I think…I love you Felix."

I fondled the film canister through my pants pocket, a reciprocal declaration stirring in my chest. I considered letting it out, wondering if it might actually be true. But at that precise moment, a snap resounded in the kitchen, followed by a panicked scrabbling noise. I stared at Zoe, then hurried out to the kitchen, throwing open the cupboard under the sink. "Shit."

"What?" Zoe asked, coming out a moment later in one of my shirts.

"There's nothing there."

Zoe looked relieved. "It got away?"

"Not exactly."

"I don't understand." She squatted beside me and peered into the cupboard. "Where's the trap?"

"It must have dragged it into the hole with it."

"Could it do that?"

"It's a big hole."

We stared at the cupboard for a minute.

"What are you going to do?" Zoe asked.

"I'm not sure."

I was less concerned with the fate of the rat than its timing. I'd been on the brink of telling Zoe that I loved her. The words had been in my mouth, and the trap had stopped me. If the rat had been killed outright, I would have taken it as a clear warning not to move in together. If it had escaped, I might have seen it as a more hopeful sign. But this quasi-escape to what in all likelihood would be a slow death in the walls was harder to interpret. I gave Zoe a strained smile, feeling an almost fatherly affection as I looked at her, standing there in my oversized shirt. "Okay," I said. "I'll start packing."

CHAPTER TEN

I was able to walk most of my things over to Zoe's apartment, one box at a time. The superintendent came out of her unit to watch in silence, arms crossed. Once I'd cleared out everything I could carry, I dropped my key in her mailbox, leaving my damage deposit to cover the cost of removing my larger pieces of furniture and repairing the hole in the bathroom wall. The last I saw of the superintendent, she was standing at the building's front door, looking not at me, but at the sky, with a haunted expression.

At Zoe's place, I immediately carved out a workspace for myself in the kitchen and started to write. When she wasn't on her own computer, Zoe skulked around, trying not to make too much noise. I took to wearing earplugs to shut out the sound of her typing or shifting in her chair or nibbling dry cereal, but the knowledge of her constant presence in the apartment was impossible to erase. In bed, she remained passive and undemanding, never failing to accommodate me, but never showing any outward signs of pleasure. Every so often, I checked the penis album, and found that she was still collecting photos.

The pictures I'd stolen from my father's look-alike remained hidden in their canister, tucked in the hip pocket of whatever pants I happened to be wearing. I hadn't brought them to a developer, fearing they'd know the film wasn't mine, but I touched the canister often as I struggled to find my way into my third book, erasing and rewriting the opening paragraph hundreds of times, telling myself that when I got that much right, the rest would come. One morning, after weeks of failure, I'd finally begun to close in on a solution, when a tap on my shoulder broke the spell.

"What?" I snapped, tearing out my earplugs.

"Sorry," Zoe said. "I just wanted to tell you that we're out of milk."

"So?"

"Well, I've been sick all day, and I was hoping you could..."

She was hunched over in a flannel nightdress, looking paler than usual. Anxiety gnawed my gut at the thought of going out, but I felt bad for not noticing she was sick and reluctantly agreed to run the errand. On the way to the corner store, I paused in front of a one-hour photo mart. A businessman weaved around me. "Point of no return," he muttered into his cellphone. I watched him disappear into the crowd, then looked at my uncertain reflection in the photo mart window and stepped inside. A shifty-eyed Eastern European woman took the stolen film from me and I emerged a minute later with an incriminating stub. For the next hour, I walked the streets under an overcast sky, trying to lose a dark car with tinted windows that seemed to be shadowing my every move. I returned to the photo mart, expecting to be tackled at the door by police, or at the very least, confronted by the woman who'd developed the film, but she gave me the photos indifferently and returned to her magazine. Resisting the urge to tear the envelope open then and there, I brought it back to the apartment and tucked it under my shirt on the elevator ride to the sixteenth floor. Boris barked when I came in and I angrily shushed him. Zoe stepped out of her room, looking relieved.

"What is it?" I asked.

"You've been gone a long time."

"Sorry," I said, trying to keep the envelope under my shirt from crinkling.

She looked at my empty hands. "Where's the milk?"

"Shit. I forgot."

"You forgot? What were you doing all this time?"

I sighed. "I'll go back, all right?"

"You don't have to yell at me. I'm just wondering where you went."

"I'm not yelling. I said I'd go back." Everything about her annoyed me: her sunglasses, her wild hair, her wounded look.

She shook her head. "It's fine. I don't need it that badly."

I gave a harsh laugh and threw up my hands. "Then why did you send me out in the first place?" Zoe faced me impassively, her eyes impossible to see. I wanted to snatch the sunglasses from her face and snap them in two. "I need to go the bathroom," I said, stumbling over Boris on my way down the hall. "Christ! This fucking place!"

I locked the bathroom door behind me, then pulled out the envelope with shaking hands and sat on the lid of the toilet, feeling as if I were holding an innocuous-looking pouch of anthrax. After a moment of indecision, I ran my finger along the top flap to release the glue. A second smaller envelope was tucked inside the first and I pulled it out.

A tentative knock came at the door. "You okay in there?"

"I'm fine!"

I waited for Zoe's footsteps to recede before carefully taking out the photos.

The first few were generic landscape shots. Ocean and sky, nothing remarkable on the surface, but I lingered on them, looking for an entry point to the photographer's mind. Pictures of an empty beach gave way to snapshots of families: parents and children in a playground, evidently unaware of the camera. Then came photos of trees, lawns and houses. I had the sense of a journey, as if the photographer were going somewhere. Halfway through the pile, I suddenly stopped, staring at a picture of my old apartment building. The next photo was taken in the lobby. Then came shots of the stairwell, the hallway leading up to my unit, and the outside of my shut apartment door. Boris raked his claws down the bathroom door.

"Jesus!" I shouted. "Can I get a minute to myself?"

I could hear Zoe scolding the dog and leading him away. The next photo showed my apartment from the inside.

"No," I moaned.

I shuffled through multiple shots of the galley kitchen, the living room and the bathroom. The photographer came to my half-open bedroom door and I braced myself for some sinister conclusion: a shot of me sprawled unconscious on the bed, a knife at my throat. But the bedroom was just as empty as all the other rooms. The final photo on the roll showed the view from my bedroom window at midday: the parking lot, the low-rise, Zoe's building just visible in the background, her window a pinprick of darkness.

I put the photos away and made a show of flushing the toilet, then hid the envelope in a cupboard under some towels. Zoe had retreated to the bedroom with Boris, both of them sitting in front of her computer. I went to the living room window and tried to find my old apartment in the distance. With no point of reference, the buildings all looked identical.

"Everything okay?" Zoe asked, eyes locked to her monitor.

"Yeah," I said. "I'm sorry."

"It's fine."

"No, it isn't. I shouldn't have spoken to you like that."

"Forget it... Someone phoned for you when you were out, by the way."

"Who?"

"A man. He said he wanted talk about your book."

"Which book?"

"I don't know."

"How did he get this number?"

"I assumed you'd given it to him," she said, typing steadily.

I looked at the phone on the coffee table. "Was it David Cavendish?"

"He didn't leave a name. Who's David Cavendish?"

"No one." I had no memory of giving David Zoe's number. "Did he say anything else?"

"No."

Whether or not David had been the one to call, I'd been thinking about getting in touch with him, hoping to get some feedback on my new project. I found his number in my email, scribbled it on my hand, and made sure I had change for the payphone, before grabbing my keys. "I'm going out," I said to Zoe.

She stopped typing and looked at me. "Again?"

"I'm getting your milk."

"I told you, you don't have to do that."

"Of course I do," I said, and left the apartment.

» » »

The restaurant was unnecessarily dark, a long and windowless space, lit only by flickering candles. I felt completely exposed at my small table in the middle of the room, unnerved by the figures shifting and murmuring around me. I finished my drink in one long swallow without knowing what it was, only that it burned on its way down. On the far side of the restaurant, a corridor with an unusual number of doors reached back into darkness. A large man with a moustache emerged from one of the doors and walked towards me. It took me a moment to recognize him.

"Still no food?" David asked, sitting down.

"Doesn't look that way," I said vaguely.

"Trust me, it'll be worth the wait. The head chef's an artist. People come from all over the country for this stuff." He crossed his legs and leaned back. "So about this book of yours, Felix. Frankly, I'm surprised that you came to me, after everything that's happened. You really put me in a tight spot, cutting off all communication like that."

"I was having a hard time."

"I gathered."

"My father had just died."

David's jaw went tight. "I'm sorry. Why didn't you tell me?"

I shrugged. "It's not important."

"Well, are you all right now?"

"Yes. I'm living with someone."

"Hey, that's great! You should have brought her along."

"Yeah…she's not really a people person."

"Match made in heaven," David observed with a grin.

I had a sudden impulse to punch him in the mouth.

"So the proposal you sent me." He tugged on his earlobe. "I have to say, I'm not quite sure what to make of it. There are some, shall we say…plausibility issues. And your protagonist isn't exactly sympathetic."

I nodded, thinking I never should have called him.

"A loser," he said, pressing home the point. "And the way he sees women? A little tone-deaf, wouldn't you say? I don't know if you've noticed, but women are having something of a moment right now."

I started to defend myself but David kept talking.

"I'm not saying you can't write about sex. But it's going to be difficult. Women have a perspective too, you know."

"I understand that."

"Do you? The women in your books aren't real, Felix. They're ideas. Symbols."

"I—"

"How are you doing over here?" a waitress in a short black skirt interrupted, suddenly appearing at our table.

David gave her a wolfish grin. "Ravenous."

The waitress ignored him, directing her frozen smile at me.

"Um..." I shifted in my chair. "I'm good."

"Great! Your food will be out in just a minute."

She walked off and David's eyes lingered on her behind. He leaned back, looking gloomy. "Irony," he said.

"What's that?"

"Your proposal. It's loaded with irony. Just think about how passive your hero is. He can't even womanize properly. He never takes charge of his situation. Things just happen to him."

"Isn't that what life's like?" I asked.

David gave me a puzzled smile. "No," he said. "It's not." His expression grew serious. "Felix, are you sure that this is the book you want to be writing right now?"

I didn't know how to answer that question. For me, when writing went well, it happened under almost trancelike conditions, as if I were transcribing someone else's words. Whether or not it was the book I wanted to write was beside the point. It was the book I'd been given.

"Have you ever considered writing something a little less... personal?" David asked. "Historical fiction? Maybe a good mystery?"

As he continued to suggest alternate directions for my career, a couple sat down at a table in a far corner of the restaurant. The man had his back to me, but I had a clear view of his red-headed companion. The longer I stared at her, the more familiar she appeared. If it really was Jasmine, she'd grown out her hair since I last saw her and adopted a new style, dressed in a kimono-like top and dark slacks, chopsticks either holding her hair in place or imbedded in it for effect. From behind, the man looked much older than her, sitting with an elbow hooked over the back of his chair and one hand on the table, palm down, pointing in her direction. He seemed to have said something funny, as Jasmine (I was certain it was her now) nodded and laughed.

"Something to think about anyway," David was saying. "Obviously, I'm not inside your head. Only you can say what really excites you. But I feel like a change of direction could be helpful."

Jasmine touched her companion's hand and an invisible vise tightened around my throat.

David swept back his hair. "I've upset you."

"No," I said, keeping my eyes on Jasmine's table.

"Then why are you so quiet?"

"I'm always quiet."

The room was stifling. The man took Jasmine's hand and turned it over, running his fingers over the lines of her palm, as if reading her future.

"For Christ's sake," David said, loudly, "what's so interesting back there?" He twisted around and Jasmine's eyes flicked up, landing on me for a moment before dodging away. "Do you know that woman?"

"No," I muttered.

Jasmine said something to her companion, who twisted around to look at us exactly as David had looked at them a moment before. My face went cold. It was my father's double. The photographer with the truck. He wore a nicely tailored sport coat, his shirt unbuttoned to reveal a thatch of grey chest hair and a pendant on a thin gold chain. I couldn't gauge his precise expression in the dim light, but he looked amused, as if Jasmine had just said something disparaging about me.

David cleared his throat. "Uh...Felix?"

My father's double turned to Jasmine and made a seesawing motion with his hand. She nodded and laughed again.

"I have to go," I announced.

"Hey." David spread his hands. "I'm sorry if I offended you.

You want to keep writing books about yourself? Knock yourself out."

I stood abruptly, jostling the table, making the cutlery clatter.

The restaurant felt static, unnaturally quiet. I had the sense of walking through a painting, past suggestions of people, towards the only possible exit: the dark corridor beside Jasmine's table. Neither she nor the man she was with seemed aware of my approach—Jasmine frowning at a wine list, while he looked at his watch. I veered towards them at the last second, coming up on the man from behind and hissing in his ear: "I know who you are."

The man jumped, nearly falling out of his chair. I'd never been that close to him before and was surprised by how little he actually resembled my father, his jaw stronger than Dad's, his nose more prominent, his eyes more symmetrical. I could feel Jasmine staring at me, but remained focused on the man. "Who sent you?" I demanded. "Why did you take those pictures?" I grabbed his arm, then stopped, registering his baffled (and terrified) expression. The more I studied his face, the less sure of myself I became. The woman was on the verge of tears. She looked nothing like Jasmine—several inches taller and at least ten years older. All they had in common was the hair. Everyone in the room was watching. David should have been furious, but from his place at the table, he looked strangely pleased. I let go of the man's arm and strode off down the corridor, passing door after door until I came to a flight of stairs that led to what looked like the main exit. The handle was solid and reassuring. I swung the door open and emerged onto a busy street: headlights streaming past under a purple sky, the air cool and bracing, a line of well-dressed people standing under a glowing marquee across the road. I walked away from the underground restaurant, feeling as if the world were being hastily assembled in front of me, the ground solidifying an instant before I stepped onto it. As I walked, my panic began to fade. None of it was real. Not the restaurant or Jasmine or David. Not the street under my feet. And not me. Least of all me. *Yes*, a voice in my ear confirmed. "Well?" I said out loud. "What do I do now?" *Close your eyes*, the voice said. I obeyed, walking blind for five, ten, twenty paces without stumbling. I opened my eyes, recalling David's broad smile. He wanted action, I'd give him action. I shut my eyes for another twenty paces. Forty. Sixty. I may not have known exactly what to do next, but sensed something protecting me, guiding me, leading me exactly where I needed to go.

» » »

"Do you mind if I ask what you're doing?" Zoe asked.

I looked up from the funnel of concentric circles sliding across the screen of my sleeping laptop. "Sorry?"

"You've been staring at that screensaver for a long time," she said, her eyes almost visible through her tinted lenses thanks to the strong sunlight coming through the kitchen window. "I thought you might have gone somewhere."

"Somewhere?"

"In your mind."

"I was thinking about my work."

"Oh. Okay."

I returned my eyes to the screen, then looked at her again. "How long is a long time?"

"Well..." She poured herself a cup of coffee and dumped in three spoons of sugar. "I've been in and out all afternoon and you've hardly moved. I was starting to wonder if there was...I don't know. Someone else."

I stroked the trackpad to wake my computer, then opened my word processor and scrolled through a list of document files. Zoe lingered in the kitchen with her coffee until I looked up at her again.

"Sorry," she said. "It's just...if there was someone else, you'd tell me, wouldn't you?"

"There's no one else."

Looking less than reassured, Zoe shuffled away and left me to my work. When I heard her start typing in the next room, I minimized my word processor and opened a browser. Ever since the incident in the restaurant, I'd been haunting adult webcams, asking anyone who would listen if they remembered the website with the coloured doors, and more specifically, a redhead with a certain tattoo. Without exception, the performers either ignored me or ejected me from their chatrooms, and this afternoon was no different. I logged onto site after site, interrogating performers and users until my first lead finally came, not from the petite blonde gyrating on my screen, but from a fellow user who went by the name John Ayes.

You trying to find Jasmine?

I looked up from my screen, listening to the soft clacking of Zoe's keyboard.

Yes, I wrote back. A long pause followed.

I know where she is.

Online?

Real world.

An urgent, whirring rhythm started up in my head. *Where?*

Not so fast. I want something in return.

What?

Email would be more secure. Your address?

I gave him an anonymous email address I'd previously set up and he disappeared from the room. I navigated to my inbox, but found no new messages waiting. I refreshed. Nothing changed. For the rest of the night, I sat in front of the laptop, compulsively refreshing my inbox, until Zoe poked her head in around two in the morning, "Coming to bed?"

The walls swam when I looked up at her. "Not just yet."

"Work's going well?"

"Uh-huh."

She left the room, defeated. I hit the refresh button. Once she'd fallen asleep, I migrated out to the living room with my laptop, not wanting to take my eyes off the screen for a moment. I must have eventually fallen asleep, as I woke on the loveseat with a stiff neck, morning sun in the windows, my hibernating laptop on the coffee table. I touched the trackpad, adrenaline jolting me fully awake as I saw a new, unopened message at the top of my screen. I opened it and found three short lines of text:

Café Brew Ha Ha @ 9:30 AM.

$500 for full contact information.

Look for the red shirt and white hat.

I checked the time on the laptop. Nine-fifteen. As far as I knew, there was only one Café Brew Ha Ha in the city, a short walk from Zoe's apartment. Zoe was snoring softly in the bedroom, a bottle of sleeping pills on the nightstand beside her. I grabbed my wallet and keys from the coffee table and hurried down to the elevator. A small boy was standing beside the closed door, having already pushed the down button. He couldn't have been older than five, but seemed perfectly comfortable with no adult supervision. The door opened and we climbed on together, riding down to the lobby in silence, him watching me with interest, as if expecting me to do something exciting. At the main level, I jumped off and jogged down the street to an ATM. My daily limit was five hundred dollars. I withdrew it all, then jammed the wad of twenties into my pocket and sprinted the last few blocks to the café. A chime sounded as I staggered through the door, breathing hard. The place was deserted. I ordered a coffee from the kid behind the counter and sat down at a table to wait. No red shirt appeared. No white hat. A full hour went by and not a single person walked through the door. I gave up and left the café, certain I was going to find a second, mocking email in my inbox when I got back. Down the street, I saw the little boy from the elevator on the crowded sidewalk, still alone, looking like he knew exactly where he was going.

I headed in the opposite direction as him, back to our building, where I let myself in and stopped. A police officer stood waiting in the lobby. I nearly lifted my hands, thinking he'd come about Kim's window or the stolen film or something far worse that I couldn't remember doing, but he hardly glanced at me, occupied with a frantic woman who was sobbing to anyone that passed: "My son! Have you seen my son?" I excused my way through the small crowd that had gathered, saying nothing about the boy I'd seen on the street. He hadn't been in any danger. He hadn't looked scared. For all I knew, he had a perfectly good reason for wanting to get away from the woman. By the time I reached the elevator, I'd almost convinced myself that I was doing something noble by not telling her where he was. Three other tenants climbed on with me and the door closed. "Scary," one of them said and I nodded vaguely, watching the broken display above the door flicker. At the sixteenth floor, I stepped off, and hurried down the hall to Zoe's apartment (I still couldn't think of it as *our* apartment), throwing the deadbolt behind me and locking the chain for good measure.

Zoe hadn't moved, still in bed, one arm flung out to the side, as if receiving an injection. No message had come from John Ayes. I'd just started writing him an angry email, when a quiet knock broke my train of thought. I looked at the door. The knock came again, a little louder.

"Hello?" a man called from the hall,

Zoe didn't have a spyhole, but the voice sounded authoritative—polite but insistent. Assuming it had something to do with the missing boy, I undid the locks, inwardly rehearsing what I was going to say. If pressed, I would have to admit that we'd ridden down to the lobby together, but no one could have possibly known that I'd spotted him later on the street.

I opened the door, surprised to find one of the tenants from the elevator waiting in the hall, a thin young man, with wire-rimmed spectacles and a bright orange T-shirt under a brown leather vest. "Yes?" I said.

The man grinned. "Dramatic scene."

"I'm sorry?"

"Boy goes missing. Cops show up. Unexpected." He stepped across the threshold, forcing me back with his casual momentum. He wandered over to the window and peered down at the street. "Nice view."

"Can I help you?" I stammered, still standing by the open door.

The man turned with a slow smile. "I think the question is, can I help *you*?" If he'd noticed Zoe on the bed in the next room, he didn't show it. He sat down on the loveseat, knees apart, forearms on his thighs.

"What do you want?" I asked.

"Just a little conversation."

I shook my head. "I don't know what—"

"Is this your hardware?" He nodded at my open laptop on the coffee table, the email I'd been working on clearly visible. "*Dear John*," he read out loud. "*You are a useless, pathetic, good for nothing troll...*" He leaned back, looking amused. "Well, that's not very nice."

"What are you going to do?" I asked.

"I told you. I'm just here to talk."

I still hadn't closed the door. Physically, he was hardly imposing, but his dead-eyed smile made me reconsider forcing him to leave. "We could have talked at the café," I said. No point pretending I didn't know who he was.

He nodded. "True. But I like to know who I'm talking to in a situation like this. I wanted to meet..." He picked up a power bill from the coffee table and looked at it. "Felix Mallory."

"Why?" I asked, faintly.

"Why don't you shut the door."

It was more of a command than a suggestion, and I obeyed with a brief glance at the bedroom, unable to see the bed from where I was standing.

"You know,"—the man propped his feet on the coffee table—"you should really be more careful about your online interactions. You got lucky this time. You could have been talking to anyone. The cop downstairs, for instance. You looked a bit spooked by him."

"I haven't done anything."

"Of course you haven't. We're just two regular guys having an innocent conversation...Did you get the money, by the way?"

"Yes," I said.

He looked impressed. "You really want to find this girl, don't you?"

I looked him in the eye for the first time and his smile opened, revealing rows of blunt white teeth.

"Do you mind if I ask what you plan on doing when you find her?"

I looked away and he chuckled.

"Well...I'm sure you'll think of something." He pulled a slip of paper from the pocket of his vest and held it out between two fingers.

"What's that?" I asked.

"The answer to your prayers..." He waved the paper. "Redhead stripper. Hummingbird tattoo. Only her real name isn't Jasmine, it's—"

"Angela," I whispered.

He looked surprised, then his grin came back, wider than ever. "Give the man a cigar."

I pulled out my wallet and he held up his hands.

"Oh, I don't want your money. That was just to see if you were serious."

"So what do you get out of it?" I asked, confused.

"Just the pleasure of helping a fellow...enthusiast. We're solitary animals, Felix. We'll never be friends. People like us don't have friends. But that doesn't mean we can't look out for each other." He held out the paper again. I told myself he was wrong. We weren't the same. But in that moment, it felt as if he knew me better than I knew myself. I stepped into his orbit. Our fingertips brushed with a snap of static electricity, and the paper changed hands.

"Well," he said. "I guess that's everything." He got up and strolled over to the door, then turned back. "Oh, there was one last thing. I wouldn't consider this a condition as much as a request. A professional courtesy, if you like. If you find her. *When* you find her. Take pictures. You know where to send them..." He dropped me a theatrical wink. "I like to watch."

Before I could respond, the man had slipped out of the apartment and shut the door quietly behind him. I stared at the door for quite some time before locking the bolt and chain. If it weren't for the paper in my hand, I'd have wondered if he'd really been there at all.

"Hey."

I spun round, stuffing the note into my back pocket. Zoe had shuffled out of her room in her sunglasses and an ankle-length bathrobe, her hair wilder than usual. "Did you make coffee?" she asked.

"I...No, not yet."

She yawned and gave me a bleary smile. "Everything all right?"

"Yes," I said, mechanically.

Boris padded out of the bedroom. It occurred to me that he hadn't made a sound the whole time the man had been there.

"How long have you been up?" Zoe asked.

"Not long."

She looked around the room with a frown. "Were you on the phone a minute ago?"

"No."

"That's weird. I thought I heard you talking."

She plodded into the kitchen, as Boris sniffed around the sofa.

"No," I muttered quietly, fireworks thudding in the right hemisphere of my brain. "It wasn't me."

CHAPTER ELEVEN

I should have been used to the gaps in time, but this felt different. I was on my feet in pitch darkness, with no point of reference, nothing to anchor me to any specific location. A sudden flash of light illuminated a face, inches from my own, and I staggered back from what I belatedly recognized as my reflection in a pane of glass.

"Zoe?" I called out in the renewed darkness.

I felt my way through rooms filled with strange objects: a lawnmower, a pile of firewood, a body sprawled on the floor. The body groaned, and I knelt down to touch fur. A glint of bared teeth. I drew my hand back and stood up. "Zoe?" I called again, my voice edged with fear. My fingers grazed a wall, and I stepped through an open doorway. Light flashed again, briefly illuminating Zoe's photo album, lying open on the living room floor, filled with the pictures of my old apartment. I reached for the book, but my hand closed around a folded piece of paper. I lifted the paper, straining to read what appeared to be John Ayes' handwriting.

Keys rattled in the door and Boris barked.

"Shut up," I said. He barked again and I aimed a kick at him. "I said, shut up!"

The door swung open and Zoe's silhouette appeared in the doorway. "Felix?"

"What?" I shouted back.

"What's going on? Why is it so dark in here?"

Zoe flipped a switch and I winced, shielding my eyes from the sudden light. Boris charged over to greet her, whining, tail pumping. She dropped a suitcase and bent to hug him. "Hi boy! How are you doing? Oh, I missed you so much!" I looked out the window. Lightning flickered in the night sky, a hard rain pummeling the street. Zoe stood up and grinned. "Is that for me?" She was looking at the paper in my hand—not a note after all, but a twenty-dollar bill. I jammed the money into my pocket and took a step back.

"Felix?" Zoe said.

"Sorry. I just need to..." I pointed to the bathroom and hurried inside. I pulled out the paper. It had changed again, this time into a photograph of my old kitchenette—a large pot in the foreground on top of the stove. I held the picture up, noticing something I hadn't before: a distinct reflection of the photographer in the pot's curved metal. I brought it closer to my face, seeing not the man with the truck, but a woman, with fiery red hair.

When I came out of the bathroom a few minutes later, Zoe was sitting on the loveseat.

"My flight was good," she said. "In case you were wondering."

"How was your flight?" I asked, numbly.

She frowned at me. "What is going on with you?"

I held up a finger. "Just...give me a minute." I went into the kitchen, a steady drumbeat in my ears. I opened and closed cupboards at random, looking for something I couldn't name. I turned, shouting in surprise to find Zoe standing inches away.

"Christ! Don't do that!"

"Sorry."

I abandoned the cupboards and started opening drawers. One was filled with tea towels. Another held batteries, rubber bands, and pens. I jerked open the cutlery drawer and stared at the knives.

"What are you looking for?" Zoe asked.

I exhaled and shut the cutlery drawer.

"Babe?" she said. "Are you mad at me?"

"No." I bent over, trying to catch my breath. "I just...I didn't realize you'd left."

"I've been gone for two weeks."

"Wow. Okay."

"Maybe you need to lie down."

I straightened, slamming my head into the corner of an open cupboard door. "Fuck!" I shrieked, holding my head. "Motherfucking fuck!"

Zoe stared at me (or seemed to, behind the sunglasses). I checked my hand for blood, wished there was blood, but it came away clean. I stalked out of the kitchen, stumbling over Boris who'd fallen asleep in the living room, then grabbed my keys, and left the apartment altogether. The boy who'd gone missing was down by the elevator again, this time with his mother, who gave me a hostile look and pulled her son closer. I opened the door to the stairwell and started to climb, hauling myself up flight after flight until I came to a barred door with a sign reading "Maintenance only." Breathing hard, I shouldered the door open. No alarm sounded, nothing to keep me from stepping out onto the flat asphalt roof.

The rain was gone, the roof completely dry. A weak orange light mounted beside the door buzzed. A breeze tugged me forward. As I approached the roof's edge, the asphalt underfoot looked grainy and unreal. The low guardrail would have been easy to climb over. If I jumped, it would take less than five seconds to hit the ground. The street below looked like a poor rendition of an actual street, like something a child might draw. Far off, in the direction of the ocean, I could see a handful of small lights that must have been boats. I reached in my pocket, unsurprised to find that John Ayes' note had returned. I still hadn't looked at it directly, sensing that the information it contained was dangerous, that in reading it, I would become someone different. Of course, that did nothing to change my desire to see Jasmine, to wind myself around her like a strand of DNA. Before I could reconsider, I opened my hand and let the breeze sweep the paper away.

A crushing pain gripped my chest as I watched it vanish.

Back in the apartment, Zoe was putting on dinner. Not only had she changed her clothes, she'd cut her hair. Boris was sitting at her feet, waiting for a stray morsel of food to hit the floor.

"I'm sorry," I said, miserably.

She kept her eyes on the lettuce she was cutting. "About what?"

"Everything."

She laughed. "Is that all?"

"I don't mean to be this way."

She peeled the plastic film off a frozen lasagna and tucked it into the oven. "It's fine."

"No, it isn't. I hate the way that I treat you."

"So treat me better," she said, simply.

"I don't know if I can."

"Okay."

"Okay?" Annoyance flared up in me. "*Okay*? Christ, Zoe. What if I knocked you across the room right now? Would that be okay too?"

"You'd never do that."

"How do you know?"

"I just do."

I pushed the heels of my palms into my eyes until stars came. I felt like I'd made Zoe out of cardboard and propped her up with a stick, like I was alone in the kitchen, talking to myself. But when I dropped my hands, I could see that she was crying behind the dark lenses, an actual person in real pain—pain that I'd caused. "Hey, don't," I said. "Oh, Jesus.

I'm sorry…" I put my arms around her and she buried her face in my chest, sobbing. I stared at the oven timer over her shoulder, watching the numbers tick down. The floor vibrated under us, as if from a small magnitude earthquake. I was about to ask Zoe if she'd felt it when I found myself swept off in a roar of colour and sound, a cataract of time ripping through the apartment, bringing me to a gentle hill studded with grave markers. The rectangular stone in front of me held my mother's name and the span of her life. Nothing else. No poem or commentary on the woman she'd been. A second marker sat beside the first, etched with my father's name and birthdate, the death date blank. Dad was on his back in the grass in front of his marker, directly above the spot where he would eventually be buried, his hands behind his head. A warm breeze blew through the graveyard, disturbing his thinning hair. Eileen had wandered off, playing some game that involved leaping over the markers.

"It's funny," Dad said, "how suddenly it happens. One second you're up here, the next…" He trailed off, staring at the empty sky.

I watched Eileen, wishing I could join her.

"Somewhere up there," Dad said, "there's a meteor the size of a mountain. Bigger than the one that killed off the dinosaurs. Tumbling through space, headed straight for us. We all know it's coming. We just don't know when. But what if we did? What if we knew the exact moment it was going to hit? What would it change? What would we do differently?"

I shifted uncomfortably, feeling that he shouldn't have been talking to me this way, as if I were an adult. Eileen was practicing her cartwheels now, spinning off through the graveyard like a flywheel.

"Nothing," Dad answered himself. "Absolutely nothing. We'd do all the same things. Make all the same mistakes…" He frowned. "I wonder if it's all still back there somewhere. Everything that happens. Everything we do. Like a groove on a record. Only we can't see it because we're stuck riding the needle."

Little white moths fluttered around us in the grass. I turned my face to the sky. When I looked down, Dad was watching me with a bemused expression.

"Do you remember your mother?" he asked.

I shook my head.

"That's probably for the best. You remind me of her so much sometimes, it's scary..."

I understood by the way he said it, that this wasn't entirely a good thing. He stood up and brushed the grass from the seat of his pants. We could hardly see Eileen anymore, but Dad didn't seem concerned. Feeling suddenly lonely, I slipped my hand into his. He allowed the contact for a few seconds, then pulled away and gave me an awkward pat on the shoulder. "Enough of that," he said. "It's time to go home."

Another jolt brought me back to the kitchen, with Zoe in my arms, the oven timer running down. I had the sense of being in multiple places at once: the kitchen, the graveyard, my old apartment, the school bathroom with Chad. I held Zoe at arm's length, tunneling into that one specific moment. I took off her glasses. She gazed at me steadily, and I noted that her eyes were green.

"I love you," I said.

The oven timer went off and suddenly Zoe wasn't in my arms anymore, but on the other side of the room, taking the lasagna out of the oven. She set it on the stovetop beside a large knife. She had her sunglasses on again. I couldn't remember returning them to her, or for that matter, if she'd told me she loved me back. I sat down at the kitchen table and we ate in silence, as one does after someone has died. Then we were in bed, Zoe underneath me, naked, letting me make love to her, Boris sprawled on the other half of the bed. At the moment of my climax, he shifted and heaved a long sigh. I lay still a moment, breathing hard, before withdrawing from Zoe, who gave me a peck on the shoulder and headed for the bathroom. I stayed where I was, listening to the shower, thinking about the note I'd tossed off the roof, wondering if it was too late to reclaim it. Zoe came back with one towel snugged up to her armpits and another turbaned around her head. She sat down on the bed and I waited for her to ask me what I was thinking about.

"What are you thinking about?" she said.

My face muscles tensed. "Nothing."

"You must be thinking about something."

I sighed. The bed felt too small for the three of us, Boris stretched out to claim far more than his share. "I am truly thinking about nothing."

Zoe made a worried noise. Now, she'd want to know if the sex was all right.

"Was that okay?" she asked.

"It was great," I said stiffly.

Next, what was wrong.

Worry lines appeared above her dark glasses. "What's wrong?"

"Nothing."

Boris lifted his head and watched me warily. *You seem angry.* The words flashed through my head an instant before Zoe spoke them: "You seem angry."

Dread opened in my stomach. Boris and I stared at one another.

Do you really love me? The question seemed to come from the dog.

"Do you really love me?" Zoe said half a second later.

"Of course," I said, speaking to Boris now.

Why?

"Why?"

Boris growled softly.

Zoe put a hand on his back. "What is it, Bo?"

"It's me," I said. "He's growling at me."

The next bit of conversation came to me in a rush.
He's not growling at you.
Yes, he is.
Why would he growl at you?
Because he knows what I'm thinking.
I thought you weren't thinking about anything.
Well I fucking lied, didn't I?
Boris was staring at me intently, his hackles up. "He's not growling at you," Zoe said.

"Yes, he is," I replied, helplessly.

"Why would he—"

With an effort that hurt, I tore myself out of the scene and bolted from the room, hearing Boris's substantial bulk hit the floor an instant later. His claws raked the hardwood. Naked, I sprinted through the living room and skidded into the kitchen, Boris close on my heels. The butcher's knife was lying on the stove, where Zoe had left it. I snatched it up and whirled to face Boris as he charged into the room, tongue lolling out the side of his mouth, eyes bright and happy. He wasn't attacking. He was playing. Either he didn't see the knife or he didn't have the sense to fear it. As he launched himself at me, some weird reflex made me tighten my grip on the handle. The blade sank deep into his neck. He reared back, yelping, blood spraying the walls as the knife slid out, still in my hand. Zoe hurried into the kitchen, in her sunglasses and towel. "No!" she yelled, seeing Boris on the floor. "No! No! No!" She threw herself over him. The life was leaving his body with surprising speed. He thrashed in her arms a few seconds before going still. Zoe cradled his head in her lap, looking at me over her sunglasses, her eyes filled with despair. I couldn't guess what she was going to say next. Nor did I want to find out. Dropping the knife to the floor, I walked past them both and headed for the door. In the hall, I punched the elevator button, stark naked and shivering, wet with Boris's blood. When the elevator didn't come,

I abandoned it and took the stairs, jogging down flight after flight, until I reached the main level, where I passed several tenants on my way through the lobby. I could see from their faces that I'd transformed into something terrifying, an animal on whom clothing would have looked absurd. A wild shriek tore its way out of my throat, flattening them against the walls. Then, hunched like a troll, genitals swinging, I gripped the handle of the front door and stepped out into the crowded street.

CHAPTER TWELVE

The head psychiatrist listened to my description of the event with an indulgent smile, nodding from time to time, as if I were telling him something entirely expected. Then he turned to the other members of the team—an intern, a psychologist, and a nurse—and talked about me for a few minutes as if I weren't in the room, using terms like *fugue state*, *paranoia, hallucinations, psychosis*. Sticky notes sectioning off different parts of my brain. Returning to me with a fatherly smile, he assured me that with the proper treatment, he could have me back to my old self within a few short weeks. And he had more good news. I hadn't hurt anyone. I'd been found roaming the streets, bloody and naked, but the blood appeared to be my own, from a gash on my hand which had since been bandaged.

"I don't understand," I said, crossing my arms in an attempt to maintain some dignity in my hospital gown and paper slippers. "What about Boris?"

"Who?"

"The dog."

"Ah," Dr. Patel said, with a faint smile. "Right. The dog."

"It was an accident." I rubbed the side of my face to quiet a spasming muscle. "He jumped at me. I didn't mean to..."

"No, I'm sure you didn't. But the thing is, Felix, the officers who brought you in sent someone to check your apartment, and they didn't find any dog there."

"Well, then Zoe must have taken him somewhere. Did they ask her?"

The other members of the team exchanged uncomfortable looks, but Dr. Patel's smile never wavered. "No," he said. "They didn't ask Zoe."

"Why not?"

"Felix." Dr. Patel leaned forward, hands clasped between his knees. "Your landlord told the police that you've been living alone in that apartment since you moved in three months ago."

"What?" I barked out a laugh. "That's crazy!"

No one else in the room was smiling. I shook my head. "Why would he say that? My name isn't even on the lease."

"Actually..." Dr. Patel picked a sheet of paper up off his desk. "Your name is the only name on the lease. I requested a copy. I thought you might like to see it."

I took the photocopied lease agreement, my eyes darting down to the signature at the bottom. "I don't...That's impossible."

"Is it?" Dr. Patel asked. "You say you've been missing time."

I rubbed the side of my face harder. "She must have taken her name off the lease. Maybe I did sign it at some point...I mean, I must have. But she was definitely living there, so..."

"After your initial story," Dr. Patel said, in that same mild tone, "the police interviewed your neighbours. None of them had any recollection of a woman matching Zoe's description ever living in that unit, or a dog for that matter. In fact, the building doesn't even allow pets."

I blinked rapidly, pushing hard at the fluttering muscle in my cheek. "I don't understand."

"There's no easy way to say this, Felix. We believe that Zoe was a mental construction. Something you built in your mind."

I crossed and uncrossed my legs, fidgeting wildly, touching my forehead, my mouth, the back of my head.

"I don't..." I said, fighting off tears, "I don't know what's happening right now..."

The nurse handed me a tissue, her face creased with pity. "Take a deep breath," she said. "Everything's going to be all right."

"But how can that even be possible?" I asked Dr. Patel. "I saw her every day. She talked to me. I touched her. We..."

Dr. Patel's indulgent smile returned. "Your mind's been telling itself a little story. A very convincing story, but a story all the same."

I shook my head, remembering the timbre of her voice, the warmth of her body. "You can't just make up another person. That's ridiculous..."

Dr. Patel looked over at the others. "I think that will be sufficient for today."

"I'm telling you—"

"We'll have plenty of time to go over all this later, Mr. Mallory. Right now, it's important that you rest."

An invisible wall went up between us as he bent over his voice-recorder, leaving the others to descend on me with helpful smiles. Back in my room, I stared at the blank little TV mounted next to my bed. A chair for visitors sat at my side, empty since I'd been admitted two days before. Above the chair, a frosted window offered plenty of light but no view. The curtain around my bed was half-shut, separating me from my roommate—a thin, white-haired man who spent most of his time humming a tune I found vaguely familiar. At the moment, he wasn't humming but whispering something I couldn't quite make out. As I strained to hear, a sturdy, cheerful-looking nurse strode in with some pills and a glass of water. "Well hello, my dear! My name's Meredith. I'll be the nurse on duty this morning. You need anything at all, just push your call button by your side there, and I'll come running, all right? Now, Dr. Patel has prescribed these for you..." She set the pills on a narrow table beside me. "You'll want to take them with food so they don't upset your tummy. I can get you some pudding or cookies, if you like."

"I'm not really hungry," I said.

"Well, how about some saltines? Just so you have something in you."

"Do I..." I lowered my voice, not wanting to sound combative. "Do I have to take those?"

She put her hands on her hips. "Dr. Patel would like you to take them."

"I understand that." My voice quavered and I tried to smooth it out, to sound reasonable. Sane. "But do I *have* to take them?"

"No one will force you to take them," Meredith said. "If that's what you're asking."

I thought about the state I'd been in when I arrived at the hospital: strapped to a gurney, naked and bellowing, fighting anyone who tried to lay hands on me, snapping at them with my teeth.

"Um...were you here on the weekend?" I asked.

Meredith shook her head. "I had the weekend off. Why do you ask?"

"No reason." I gestured at the pills on the table. "So...you think I need those?"

"Dr. Patel seems to think so," she said, diplomatically.

"What do you think?"

"I think he's very good at his job."

Her smile remained friendly, her gaze steady and calming. I felt a hard stirring of physical attraction and looked away. "I think," I said, "I'll just wait a bit. If that's okay."

"Are you sure?"

I nodded.

"All righty. Well, buzz me if you change your mind." She took the pills back and left me alone with my neighbour, who'd gone quiet. I thought he'd fallen asleep, but after a minute he started humming that same maddeningly familiar tune.

For nearly a week, Meredith brought my pills with breakfast and took them away again when I politely refused. The terms of my confinement weren't entirely clear, but I knew that the main door to the ward was locked and monitored with cameras. I could have visited the day room, but chose to remain in my own room, where my neighbour's humming had begun to grow discordant and agitated. On his daily rounds, Dr. Patel insisted that I was never going to make any progress without medication, but Meredith never pressured, lingering in the room a few minutes to talk about the weather or innocuous stories in the news. When I finally worked up the nerve to tell Dr. Patel that I intended to refuse the medication indefinitely, he sat down in the visitor's chair with my chart, looking mildly exasperated. "Do I need to remind you what brought you here?"

I didn't answer and he jotted a note in my chart.

"It's an illness, Felix. Just like diabetes or hypertension. The nature of your illness prevents you from recognizing this."

"You weren't there," I said. "You can't say for certain that it wasn't real, that there isn't some other explanation for what happened."

"What I know," Dr. Patel said, "is that you have nothing to lose by giving medication a chance."

I wasn't so sure about that.

The next morning, I woke feeling that someone had been sitting in the visitor's chair, watching me while I slept. Tiny particles of dust swirled in the narrow band of sunlight pushing through a gap in the curtains. The room was unusually quiet, the noise of faraway traffic just audible above the hiss of the ventilation system.

"Jasmine," my neighbour said, in a sudden, loud voice, as if issuing a command, as if the name were a verb, something I was being instructed to do. I stared at the curtain dividing our beds, waiting for him to say something else. Then the door opened and an orderly rolled in with our breakfasts. I shut my eyes, pretending to be asleep. Once the orderly had gone, I chewed on a piece of dry toast and watched the curtain closely.

When Meredith came in a few minutes later, I told her that I wanted to take the pills.

"That's good," she said, looking genuinely pleased.

"I *want* to," I repeated, "but I don't know if I can."

"Why not?"

I shook my head. "I'm not sure."

I couldn't bring myself to tell her that my trips though time made me feel unique, that without them, there would be nothing to separate me from the pale man. She sat on the edge of my bed and smiled. She offered no advice, no platitudes, just her simple, calming presence. "Okay," I muttered, and picked up the pills. After I'd taken them, she squeezed my hand and gave me a proud look. I flushed, absurdly pleased with myself. Before I could find the words to thank her, she stood up and carried on with her work, leaving me alone on the bed, straining to hold onto the warmth she'd briefly pressed into my hand.

» » »

For the next month, I took my pills every morning. Dr. Patel came and went, asking pointed questions, making small dosage changes based on my responses, calibrating me like a finicky machine. Gradually, the world around me felt more permanent. Time passed—slowly, predictably. My fixation on the past softened. My unimportance reasserted itself. People remained terrifying, but the intense paranoia I'd been experiencing abated.

Twice a week, I met with Dr. Howard, a distractingly attractive psychologist who favoured short skirts and high heels. Her fingers were conspicuously bare and she wore abstract little brooches that drew your eye to the exposed skin at the base of her throat, a prelude to cleavage, somehow more enticing than actual cleavage. She had a bizarre fixation on my childhood, teasing out old traumas, while I sat in a state of semi-aroused panic and responded with as few words as possible, wanting desperately to return to the quiet of my bed.

Meredith was different. She understood, or at least respected, my need to be closeted away and never tried to coax me out further than I was comfortable with. She had big motherly arms, solid thighs and a short, practical hairstyle. When she stepped into my personal space, my anxiety levels still went up, but only slightly. Unlike Dr. Patel, she treated me exactly as she would have treated someone with a physical illness, without judgment. She asked concrete questions about my life: where I grew up, where I went to school, my favourite bands and movies. She patiently listened to my halting replies, before sharing little details about herself—how she'd backpacked through Europe and Asia in her early twenties, then worked her way through college in a supermarket deli; how she was obsessed with reality television, and preferred nonfiction to fiction, and magazines to books. When she occasionally touched my arm for emphasis, the shape of her hand stayed long after she'd gone, like an impression in wet sand.

Eventually, I must have achieved whatever threshold of sanity they'd been aiming for, as Meredith arrived one morning in a celebratory mood, holding a piece of paper with Dr. Patel's sprawling signature across the bottom, informing me that he'd approved my release. I read the form closely, then set it aside.

"Isn't that great?" Meredith asked.

"Sure," I said, trying to sound enthusiastic. In the month that I'd been there, I'd grown accustomed to the hospital's countless little intrusions. I felt supported by them, taken care of. Meredith's regular visits sustained me. The prospect of stepping out of the hospital, never to see her again, wasn't just depressing, it was terrifying.

We did our ritual with the pills and she asked if I had somewhere to go.

"Of course," I said, although I'd written Zoe's landlord that very week, asking him to end my rental contract and dispose of my things however he saw fit. At the time, it had felt liberating, but now, given the fact that I didn't even have an old pair of jeans to wear, it just seemed rash. Evidently aware of my predicament, Meredith asked, "What size waist are you?"

"Thirty-four," I said.

"And shoes?"

"Ten."

"We should have something in the donations closet. I'll be right back."

She returned a minute later with an orange tracksuit and a pair of white tennis shoes, then left me alone to change. The shoes were loose, but stayed on if I laced them tight. The tracksuit fit perfectly. When Meredith swept back the curtain, I was sitting on the bed, fully dressed.

"Looking good!" she said. "You know, it's not going to be the same around here without you."

I blushed, even though I knew she must have said those exact words to every patient she'd ever discharged. The old man in the next bed was either deeply asleep or dead, his eyes shut, his mouth open.

"I don't know if I'm ready," I said, panicked.

"Oh, you're ready." Meredith gave me a confident smile. "I'm so happy for you, Felix."

I could feel her getting ready to leave the room. My throat clenched.

"Would you..." I said, and Meredith stopped at the door. The rest of the sentence tumbled out in a rush, like an eight-syllable word: "like to get a coffee sometime?"

The question was ludicrously bold. She was a nurse. I was a psych patient. Even under different circumstances, she'd have been too normal, too kind, too good for me. I nearly retracted the invitation before she could answer, but she seemed to actually be thinking about it: her mouth bunched up on one side, her hand on the open door, an eye on my neighbour. Then her usual sunny smile returned and she shrugged. "Sure. Why not."

» » »

We met a few days later in a leafy neighbourhood in the suburbs, far from my old apartment, on the patio of a café filled with retired couples and trendily dressed moms. I hadn't had a cigarette or a drink in months, and as we sat down at a small table together, I suddenly wanted both. Although my breakdown had happened in a different part of the city, any one of the people on the patio could have witnessed me naked and screaming downtown not that long before. I'd bought new clothes, but felt like an impostor in them. Meredith herself looked entirely different in street clothes—her hair teased back from her face, a generous amount of makeup rendering her almost unrecognizable. Her gently smiling face blazed across the table at me. I couldn't make eye contact for more than a second, my body vibrating as obscene levels of cortisol pumped through it.

"Can we leave?" I asked, before we'd even had a chance to sip our drinks.

"I'm sorry?"

"I'd like to go somewhere else. Do you mind?"

Meredith seemed bemused but gamely collected her things and followed me off the patio with her paper cup.

"Tables are hard for me," I explained as we walked down the sidewalk together. "I find it easier to talk to someone when we're both facing the same direction."

"I see."

"Is it the same way for you?" I asked, hopefully.

"Well, no," she admitted. "But it's fine."

We carried our drinks past a strip mall and into a small park surrounded by older two-storey homes. It was starting to get dark. I wanted to tell Meredith that she didn't have to worry, that I'd taken my medication that morning, but she looked perfectly at ease (naively so, it seemed to me) as she gazed around the park.

In the distance, a small group of boys were kicking a soccer ball around. We came to a bench and I asked if she wanted to sit.

She shrugged amiably. "All right."

We sat facing the boys. The soccer ball flew back and forth. I couldn't stop shaking.

"Where did you say you were staying again?" Meredith asked.

"The Best Western on Fifth."

"That's right. Is it nice?"

"It's okay. It has a pool."

"Oh! Do you swim?"

"No." I stared at the soccer players. "I'm sorry...I'm really nervous."

"Don't be nervous."

"Okay."

"It's nice here," Meredith said. "Don't you think?"

I nodded, tears of self-pity welling in my eyes. I couldn't see what she was seeing. The park didn't look nice at all. It looked dangerous. As the sun slipped behind the trees, one of the boys fell to the ground and the others swarmed around him, kicking. Meredith was six inches away from me at most, but felt much further. She held her cup with both hands, her back perfectly straight. "I haven't been out with a man in years," she said, confirming that this was in fact a date for her.

"Oh?" was all I could think to say.

"I was engaged. He broke it off. Since then, there hasn't seemed to be much of a point."

"Jerk," I said. "I mean, I'm sorry, but I can't imagine that. You're just so..." I trailed off, groping for the right superlative.

Meredith laughed. "Well, that's kind of you, but people aren't always the way they appear. I struggled with depression for a long time before they sorted my meds out... If there's one thing that I've learned as a psych nurse it's that none of us are immune."

"Yeah, but I'm different. I'm *really* different."

"No, Felix. You're not. If you had a window into other people's heads, I don't think you'd be so hard on yourself."

Out on the field, the fallen boy was back on his feet, unharmed and laughing. It took me a moment to realize that one of Meredith's hands was drifting towards me, crossing the space between us in slow motion. It came to a rest on my little finger.

"Is that all right?" she asked.

I glanced over, surprised to see the shadow of something I understood pass across her face, loneliness mingled with hope. "Yeah," I said. "It is."

We had our second date at Meredith's house. She lived on a narrow cul-de-sac lined with ironwoods, several kilometres from my old apartment. She picked me up from the hotel in an older sedan and we ate Indian takeout on her couch, while watching a family-oriented comedy about an eccentric old married couple. Meredith laughed at nearly every punchline, not helplessly, but dutifully, as if out of consideration for the filmmaker. Halfway through the movie, I slid my hand into hers, exactly as she'd slid hers into mine in the park. I'd never actively fantasized about her. When she'd been my nurse, it had seemed ungrateful, profane. But suddenly, sex was at the forefront of my mind. The movie ended and we watched the credits roll, still holding hands.

"Can I kiss you?" I asked, terrified.

Her eyes glittered with ironic humour. "Sure."

We lunged at different moments, butting faces like hungry birds. Through a silent, mutual agreement, we moved to her bedroom, where we undressed and crawled into bed, moving cautiously together. Later, sex would become effortless, a routine that we perfected and performed without thinking, like figure skaters. But on that first night we couldn't connect—so out of sync that my desire began to ebb away. Nothing I did could recover the situation. Eventually, I gave up and rolled onto my back.

"I'm sorry," I said.

"It's all right."

"I think maybe it's the medication."

"That can happen."

As I stared at the ceiling, Meredith sat up and took my head in her lap.

"You know," she said. "One benefit to getting older is you gain perspective. You learn that some things are more important than sex."

"Like what?" I said and we both laughed. She stroked my hair and a strange calmness came over me. Every muscle, every fibre in my body slackened as I listened to her steady breaths and the underwater sounds of her digestion. Her ample torso seemed built to accommodate the precise shape of my head. My own breath slowed, sleep coming on fast.

"That's nice," I muttered, thinking I must have slid into another delusion. This couldn't be happening. This couldn't possibly be real.

The next thing I knew, I was waking up alone in Meredith's bed, squinting in the late morning sun. I cautiously emerged from the bedroom, finding an empty house and a note in the kitchen explaining how the coffee machine worked. I set the note aside and looked out the window at Meredith's tidy back yard. Statuettes of centaurs and nymphs dotted her small flower garden, a cherry-red blown-glass hummingbird feeder suspended from a hook at the patio's edge. I'd never seen a live hummingbird before and watched the feeder hopefully for a minute, before giving up and starting the coffee machine. Meredith had left a box of cereal on the counter beside a clean bowl and spoon. I took the hint, adding a splash of milk, before carrying my breakfast out to the living room. I settled on the couch in front of the television, feeling as if I'd not only broken into a stranger's house, but stolen his identity and slept with his wife. A voice in the back of my head told me that if I cared about Meredith, I would finish my breakfast and get out. No good had ever come to anyone who'd gotten involved with me, imaginary or otherwise. And yet, I couldn't seem to remove myself from the couch. The universal remote had an interesting curve, allowing it to rest snugly in my hand. I hit the guide button and scanned Meredith's impressive cable package until I found a station running an all-day marathon of *Family Ties*. I flipped to the station and let the nostalgia wash over me, melting me back into the couch. There was something familiar about the moment. I had the sense of having dreamed it a long time ago. But I couldn't say if it would carry on pleasantly like this forever, or if it was destined to evolve into a nightmare.

CHAPTER THIRTEEN

Meredith's eyes weren't strictly brown. By the window on a sunny day, they took on an orangish hue. In the dark, they looked almost black. When she laughed they sparked with gold. When we made love, her widened pupils were depthless. Her smile was spontaneous and unstudied, and she smiled frequently, as if experiencing impossible amounts of delight throughout the day. There were no flashes of anger or sadness in those first weeks. She appeared truly content from the moment she woke to the moment she closed her eyes. I didn't know if this was her natural disposition or the work of antidepressants, but it made me want to be around her all the time, the way a student craves the company of an excellent teacher. At first, the situation felt temporary, the hotel phased out for convenience. When she came back from work I would greet her at the door with a kiss. When she left, I tried to make myself useful, tidying up, even cooking the occasional meal. My first attempt at a casserole sat Meredith back in her chair.

"Wow! That, um..." her eyes watered, and she started to cough and laugh. "That's a bit spicy."

But she appreciated the effort, and I eventually made one or two meals worthy of genuine praise. After dinner, I'd put the dishes away and we'd share the sofa for a couple of hours, watching reality shows, commenting archly on the action onscreen. Before bed, we'd brush our teeth together, taking turns spitting in the sink. Sometimes we had sex, sometimes not, but we always fell asleep with some part of our bodies touching.

On the weekends, we played card games or worked on massive jigsaw puzzles in front of the television. Occasionally, we went to the store, and I'd sit in the car while she shopped. One afternoon, she parked outside a home improvement store and turned to me with a little smile. "Why don't you come with me?"

"Uh...no, that's okay. I'll wait here."

"Oh, come on," she said, still smiling. "You're not going to make me look at paint chips all by myself, are you?"

"I..."

She laid a hand on my arm. "It'll be okay. I promise." I thought back to the phrase Kim had used on the day she first appeared in my apartment. Love-touching.

I nodded and unbuckled, getting out somewhat unsteadily and crossing the wide parking lot with my hand in Meredith's. As we wandered through the broad aisles, the gaze of strangers slipped around me, as if I was camouflaged by the woman at my side. I soon forgot myself, stunned by the way people responded to her friendly smile with smiles of their own. She steered me over to the paint department, where I offered my opinion on the rectangular cards she presented me with. When she purchased a sample pot of Corn Stalk yellow to test in the bathroom, I stood half a foot behind her—close enough to show that we were together, but far enough to leave no doubt who was in charge.

"How was that?" she asked when we got back to the car.

"Okay," I said.

She grinned. "You did good."

The next week, she took me to a florist, then a drugstore, and finally to a crowded supermarket, where I shopped for nearly half an hour before I had to leave. After that, we took in a movie, visited an art gallery, and walked along a crowded beach. Meredith never pushed me, or insisted I do anything I wasn't ready for. When she asked me one night if I had any interest in looking for work, it was a sincere question, not a demand.

I'd made her favourite quiche for dinner, and she tucked a bite into her mouth. "I was reading that more and more people are working from their homes. Telecommuting, I think it's called. Apparently, there's work out there for writers."

"I don't know," I said. "I doubt I'd make much."

"It's not about the money, Felix. It's about keeping busy. Didn't you say you get bored when I'm not around?"

I shrugged. "A little."

"So?"

The next day, when Meredith was at work, I started to put my resume together. I wasn't sure what to do about the seven-year gap in my employment history, most of which I'd spent drifting between rooming houses. My publication credits might have had some small value, but you could tell at a glance that something terrible had happened after my final year of university. I considered revising my biography, claiming to have actually graduated and worked for some defunct business. If I was lucky, I could bluff my way into a decent-paying job. I could get my driver's license so I wouldn't have to rely on Meredith to chauffeur me around. When we went to the store together, I could be the one to approach the desk, to lay down my credit card without fear. These things were possible. There was no reason they couldn't happen.

But in that moment of wild optimism, the doorbell rang. It was the middle of the day. Visitors had never arrived unannounced before. There were no packages due that I was aware of. The bell rang again and someone knocked—urgently, as if they were in trouble. I gripped my thin resume, worried that Zoe was out there, or Kim, or the wraithlike superintendent—hammering on the door with her knobbly fist. The bell rang five more times in rapid succession. Then everything went quiet. I eased over to the window and pried the curtains apart the thinnest of slivers. Two small boys in hockey jerseys were walking away from the house with bulging garbage bags. A bottle drive. I looked down at my resume, wondering how I would ever hold down a job, when a couple of seven-year-olds could make me cower.

I might have put this humiliation behind me if it hadn't been directly followed by Meredith's first real loss of patience—a stress fracture that had been building for months. She'd just come home from a gruelling fourteen-hour shift when a shout came from the bathroom, followed by an unprecedented "Fuck!" and the sound of water hitting tile. I went in and found Meredith jamming a plunger into the toilet, dirty water and shit—my shit, it had to have been—all over the floor. "Can you get me a towel, please?" she said, pumping the plunger.

I stared at the mess on the floor, a lump of fecal matter touching her clean white sock.

"Felix!" She glared at me. "A towel!"

"Right, sorry." I hurried out of the room.

By the time I got back, she appeared to have calmed down. She took the towel from me and patted at the sewage on the floor. "I'm sorry. It's been a long day. I didn't mean to take it out on you…"

"I can clean it."

"No, no, it's fine. I've seen worse at the hospital, believe me." She looked over. "Are you all right?"

I nodded. But the reproachful look she'd delivered as I hovered in the doorway doing nothing had stung. It was the exact look that Dad had always given me, a look that communicated a silent rhetorical question. *How could anyone be so stupid?* That was what she really thought of me. She'd kept it hidden better than most, but all this time she'd held me in secret contempt. And now that I'd glimpsed her true face, her true feelings, nothing could ever be the same.

A few days later, I woke to find Meredith unpacking groceries from reusable canvas bags, filling the fridge with organic produce and good-quality meat. She might have been frugal in other areas of her life, but she made an exception when it came to food. "Hello," she said cheerily. I responded with a halfhearted smile. I'd been planning what I wanted to say all night and was starting to worry that I'd lose my nerve.

"Do you want some help?" I asked.

"No, I've got this."

She finished stocking the fridge, then neatly refolded the bags, while I sat at the kitchen table, skating a salt shaker in circles. "So…I was hoping to talk to you about something. I don't quite know how to say this…"

"Did you remember to take your meds today?"

"What? Okay, see, that's exactly what I wanted to talk about."

"Your meds?"

"No, the way you look after me. It makes me feel…inadequate."

"So you took your meds."

"Yes, I took my meds."

"Good." Meredith stuffed the folded bags in a drawer and gave me a shrewd smile. "I like looking after you."

"Seriously? You come home from a twelve-hour shift and find a crappy meal on the table, some fat middle-aged guy living on your couch…"

She laughed. "Stop it."

"Don't tell me you haven't noticed me getting fat."

"As a matter of fact, I hadn't."

"I don't contribute."

"Sure you do."

It was true that I chipped in a little from the rent I got from Dad's house, but she wasn't taking me seriously, idly going through the mail while we talked.

"Don't you find it galling?" I persisted.

She made a dismissive noise, then looked up to see if I was serious. "Felix, I make good money. I love my work. The house is paid off. You give what you can. It's fine. Your being here isn't a burden. I like having you around."

"You say that like I'm a houseboy or something."

"Hey," she said, with a light frown. "Why are you trying to pick a fight?"

I slouched in my chair. Everything had been fine up to that point. I'd been making genuine progress with Meredith's help, but suddenly I wanted to take a sledgehammer to the whole thing.

Meredith sighed and set the mail aside. "Maybe it's time to make an appointment with Dr. Howard."

"No," I said quickly, remembering the psychologist's plunging necklines and naked calves, the tantalizing spot of darkness between her folded thighs. I gave my head a firm shake to banish the image. When that failed, I hit myself—nothing serious, just one good blow to the forehead with the side of my fist, the way a person might bang on an old flickering television.

"Don't," Meredith said sharply, grabbing my hand.

"It's okay," I assured her.

"No. It isn't."

But it was okay. It was exactly what I needed. If she'd have let go, I would have done it again, with a little more force. She held both my hands until the tension left them. A familiar heaviness came over me.

"Do you want to break up?" I asked, almost hopefully.

"What? No, I want you to feel better."

"This *is* better," I said. And I meant it. Compared to the state I'd been in a few months before, an occasional knock to the head didn't just feel healthy, it felt downright therapeutic. Meredith didn't seem to know what to say to that. She deserved so much better than me: a kind, gregarious man, with an unusually lighthearted disposition.

She sighed and glanced at her watch. "*Survivor*'s on in ten minutes. It's the season finale. Do you want to watch?"

I nodded, deciding that there was nothing in the world that I'd have rather been doing at that moment than watching *Survivor*.

Meredith made popcorn and I turned on the television. Dramatic theme music boomed out of the surround sound. A montage of beautiful mud-streaked people flashed across the screen. We sat on the sofa together, the popcorn bowl between us, and for the span of an hour, everything was okay.

After *Survivor*'s final tribal council, we turned off the TV and headed for the bedroom. This was the routine. For whatever reason, sex and *Survivor* always happened on the same night. We undressed in the dark—kissing the way we always kissed, touching where we always touched. Then I was on top, riding the rhythm without protection, the way Meredith had always preferred it—trusting me to withdraw in time. I started to crest more quickly than usual and stopped. Meredith encouraged me to continue with her hips and I leaned back to look at her face. Her eyes were closed. I assumed she understood the situation and quickened my rhythm, watching her closely, wondering how I could be certain that she was actually there, that this wasn't just another ghost, another fiction I'd built for myself. Pleasure flooded my body and her eyes snapped open. She stopped moving and stared at me in surprise.

"Did you just . . ?"

A terrible clarity came over me. "I thought that you wanted…"

She looked more confused than angry, our bodies still locked together, our faces inches apart.

"No," she said. "I didn't."

I lay there for a moment, wanting to reel back the last thirty seconds of my life.

Meredith put her hands on my chest. "Excuse me. I need to…"

Then she was gone: in the bathroom, with the shower running. I pulled on a pair of sweatpants and waited for her to come back, which she eventually did, wearing a fluffy bathrobe and looking more closed off than I'd ever seen her.

"Mer," I began, intending to explain that there had been no premeditation on my part, that it had happened in the heat of the moment, that I didn't even *want* kids, but she was looking around the room, frowning slightly, as if trying to remember where she'd put her keys. When her eyes finally settled on me, her expression didn't change.

"I think," she said. "I need to be alone."

I nodded, letting her know that I found her request perfectly reasonable. "Okay. I'll make a bed on the couch."

"No, I mean alone in the house."

"Oh. Okay."

"I'll call you a cab," she said. "You should get dressed." She left the room with that same distracted look, like a person confronted by some unpleasant fact that they've always denied, but secretly feared to be true.

» » »

It took three days for Meredith to find me at the Super 8. A knock came at the door and I looked out the spyhole to find her standing in the hallway with a pizza box. I opened the door and her anxious features smoothed out.

"Hey," she said. "Have you had supper yet?"

We ate together in silence, her in a cheap office chair, me on the edge of the bed. On the muted television, a satellite image of a hurricane swirled towards a fragile archipelago. "I'm sorry I sent you away," she said when we'd finished eating. "I thought you'd get in touch."

"I didn't know if you'd want me to."

"It wasn't your fault," she said, deliberately, the way a parent speaks to a child they've made the mistake of expecting too much from. "I should have been more careful. I should have asked you to use protection."

"Because I can't be trusted," I said, my eyes going from the hurricane to the half-empty pizza box on the bed.

"I didn't say that."

"But it's true. You don't know the kinds of crazy things I've—"

"Of course I do," she said with a laugh. "Do you think I'd have invited just any patient home without digging into their history? All those terrible things you thought you did...None of them happened."

"Maybe not," I said. "But they could have."

She laughed again and shook her head in exasperation. "Are you still on your meds?"

"Yes," I said, truthfully.

"Good. That's good, Felix."

After talking it over, we agreed to give the relationship another try, but a subtle shift had occurred in our three days apart, a polite distance settling between us. We still slept in the same bed, but neither one of us seemed to have any interest in sex. We treated each other with studied kindness, the way one treats a dying loved one. On my birthday, she gave me a new laptop. The extravagance of the gift took me off guard, and I thanked her in a hollow voice, thinking I had no use for it; I hadn't written a thing since I'd gotten out of the hospital. When she was at work, I connected the machine to the internet and browsed the local classifieds for affordable one-bedroom apartments, not knowing just how or when the end would come, but sensing the moment drawing near.

Then, three days before Easter Sunday, the miracle occurred. Meredith came out of the bathroom, holding a little pink wand with a blue cross on its face.

"No," I said.

She nodded, looking dazed.

"Could it be a mistake?"

She held up a second wand, with a second blue cross.

"Maybe they're defective," I said.

"They're not defective."

"You can't know that."

"Felix, I'm a nurse."

I sat down on the couch and lowered my face to my hands. "What do you want to do?" Meredith asked after a moment.

"Me?" I looked up at her. "Isn't it supposed to be your decision?"

"That's not what I'm talking about, Felix. I'm having the baby. What I'm asking is...do you want to be a part of this?"

Pain stabbed at my right temple. "I can't," I moaned, shaking my head. "I just can't."

"Okay."

"I'm sorry."

"It's all right. I understand."

"I never meant for—"

"I know."

I looked up at her uncomplicated face; the way she was standing with her shoulders defiantly square, taking it all on herself.

"I think..." I said slowly, wanting to be sure of the words this time, "that I love you, Mer."

She smiled sadly. "I'm not sure that helps us."

"What would help us?"

She thought for a moment. "In the bathroom," she said, "looking at the results, I started to cry." She raised her hands when I began to apologize. "I wasn't upset. I was happy. I'm not a young woman, you know, and I've always wanted children. I think I must have been waiting for something like this to happen. I suppose that's why I was so careless. You're a good person, Felix, whether you realize it or not, and you could make a good father. But you'd have to want it." She paused to emphasize the point. "You'd have to really want it. And if you don't, well…"

The pain in my head had begun to subside. "I don't know what I want," I admitted. "To be honest, I don't even know if this is really happening. I mean, how can I even be sure this is real?"

Still holding the positive test, Meredith gave me a weak smile. "I was just asking myself that same question."

» » »

The room was fittingly womblike—dark and quiet, the technician moving one hand over a glowing console, the other over Meredith, who lay on the examination table, her stomach glistening with jelly under the ultrasound probe. From the angle of my chair, I had a good view of everything that was happening: pale ghosts swirling on the technician's screen, as if she were communing with souls in different realm.

"There's the heart," she said, tilting her screen so we could both see the tiny fluttering organ. Meredith gave me a broad smile and I tried to smile back as the technician applied more jelly to her abdomen and shifted the probe around. "There's an arm. A hand. The spine." A camera was integrated with the machine and I could hear her printing occasional pictures of what we were seeing. She came to the head and worked to get a decent angle. In profile, the skull looked malformed and much too large, but the technician didn't seem concerned. She fidgeted with the probe and a distinct face appeared.

"Hi there," Meredith said softly.

Horror crawled up my neck. It was obvious to me that there was something wrong with the baby, the seeds of my sickness germinating inside its tiny skull.

"So," the technician said, "would you like to know the gender?"

Meredith laughed. "Well, I would. But my..." She hesitated at the designation. "Felix," she said, "would rather not."

"Well, that's fine," the technician said. "He can step outside for a minute if he'd like."

"Would you mind?" Meredith asked me.

"Um...sure."

I slunk from the room, sensing that both Meredith and the technician were glad to have me go. Out in the hall, I sat on a folding chair, fidgeting, as people in lab coats walked briskly past. Eventually, Meredith came back out, carrying a strip of captured stills from the ultrasound, not unlike the ones you get from a photo booth at the mall.

I stood up. "What happened? I thought she was going to come back and get me."

"There wasn't much left to do. Do you want to see the photos?"

"Later. I need to get out of here."

"Okay." She took my hand and led me down the hall and back out to the waiting room, past a half-dozen pregnant women accompanied by capable, confident-looking partners. The receptionist gave me an approving look, as if I were the one supporting Meredith. I followed her through the windy parking lot to the car. She got behind the wheel and I sat on the passenger side, my head against the window.

She squeezed my leg. "Thanks. I know that was hard for you."

"I'm sorry," I said, dismayed by her low expectations, my venturing into public for more than a few minutes being something remarkable.

"Don't be silly. You did fine. Here." She handed me the photos and I held them up to the light, noting the fetus's likeness to an alien being, with its massively out of proportion head and tiny limbs.

"Mer? Do you think it looks..."

"What?" she asked, pulling out of the parking lot.
"Well...normal?"
"For a four-month-old fetus? Yes. It looks pretty normal."
I tilted the photos one way then the other. "Are you sure?"
"Try not to worry, okay? Everything's fine."
"She told you the gender?"
"She did indeed." Meredith gave me a secretive smile. "I still don't understand why you don't want to know."

I put the pictures in the glove box and looked out the window at a cyclist weaving through traffic. We'd come downtown to get to the clinic and I realized that we were just now passing the coffee shop where I'd first seen Jasmine.

"Turn right up here," I said, sitting up straighter.
"Why?"
"I want to see something."

Meredith turned onto Willow Avenue, and I scanned the street for Jasmine as we closed in on my old apartment (my *only* apartment; I still thought of the high-rise unit as belonging to Zoe). I directed Meredith to the parking lot behind the building and she pulled into one of the visitors' spots. "You lived here?" she guessed. I nodded. "Which unit?"

"There." I pointed to my old balcony. The sliding door was shut, the curtains drawn. It seemed inconceivable that anyone else could be living there. I felt myself hovering just out of sight, looking down at me in the idling car. I had an impulse to go up and hammer on the door, to force my way inside and make sure that I was really gone. I glanced over at the pale man's building, but his windows were empty.

"Okay?" Meredith asked.

"Yeah," I said, somewhat reluctantly, but as she began to pull out of the parking lot, I shouted, "Stop!" so sharply that she slammed on the brakes and sent us lurching into our seatbelts.

"What is it?" she said, looking for pedestrians.

I stared at the neighbour's front yard. The oak tree that I'd climbed over in my vision of the storm (the one that had fallen across the road) was gone; not torn up by the roots, but cut, low to the ground, leaving a stump behind as wide as a kitchen table.

"Felix?"

"It's okay," I said. "Keep driving."

Back at the house, I immediately went to the bedroom to lie down. When I came out, Meredith was putting dinner on. The ultrasound pictures had found their way onto the fridge.

"Better?" she asked, and I nodded, averting my eyes from the pictures, certain the fetus—a shrunken and disfigured version of myself—had been aware of me the whole time Meredith was being scanned: glowering at the inner walls of its prison as I crouched in my chair across the room, trying to stifle my dread.

» » »

"Give me your hand," Meredith said. I gave my hand over and she placed it on her swollen abdomen. The skin felt taut and warm. At seven months, Meredith was already having trouble walking. It didn't seem possible that her body could accommodate two more months of growth. We were sitting on the sofa, a new season of *Survivor* playing. My eyes stayed on the television.

"There," she said after a minute, "did you feel that?"

"No."

"Just wait a minute."

I stifled a yawn.

"How about that?" she asked.

"Maybe. I don't know."

Something solid shoved me with surprising force and I jerked my hand back.

"Whoa!" Meredith laughed. "That was a big one."

I pictured the fetus glaring at me. "I don't think it likes me."

"Don't be silly."

"Who's being silly? That was a very clear message. Go away."

"Give me your hand again."

"That's okay. I don't want to bother it."

"You're not bothering anyone. She likes you."

I stared at Meredith.

"What?" she said. Then, realizing her mistake: "Oh. Crap."

"It's a girl?"

"That's what they tell me. Is that a problem?"

"No, not at all. I'm just…surprised." For months I'd been picturing a decidedly male creature with oversized genitals and a smashed-in boxer's face.

Meredith chuckled. "I'm sorry. It's a miracle I didn't let it slip sooner. You don't know how hard it's been. Trying to remember to call her "it" all the time."

"They were positive?"

"Well, it's never a hundred percent, but they seemed pretty sure. Especially after the last ultrasound…Here, she's moving again. Are you sure you don't want to feel?"

I tentatively returned my hand to her stomach. This time when the push came it felt gentler, more curious than angry. I kept my hand still, registering small flutters and nudges. Meredith watched me with a smile.

"Talk to her," she said.

"What?"

"Say something."

"You think she can hear me?"

"Of course she can hear you. She has ears. Go ahead. Say something."

I lowered my mouth to Meredith's stomach and hesitated.

"I don't know. It feels weird."

"Why?"

"I'm talking to your stomach."

"No, you're talking *through* my stomach. Think of it as a wall. You felt her for yourself just now. She's there, on the other side of the wall, listening."

I kept my hand on Meredith's stomach, feeling a series of little taps and jerks. I cleared my throat and put my mouth close to Meredith's navel. "Hello?"

The flutters seemed to stop.

"I think she heard you," Meredith said.

I inhaled shakily. "So...You should probably know that your father is mentally ill."

Meredith swatted me. "Stop it. Say something nice."

"Like what?"

"That's up to you."

I thought for a minute, then lowered my mouth again.

"I promise never to hurt you," I said. "I promise to protect you. To keep you safe." I said it seriously, like I was taking a binding oath. The baby remained still. I looked up at Meredith. "Was that okay?"

She put her hand on my head, smiling softly. "Yeah, that was good."

That night when I shut my eyes, the terrible goblin fetus that had been haunting my dreams for months had been replaced by a miniature version of Jasmine, suspended in a pinkly glowing ball. Her thick red hair undulated in amniotic fluid, a faint ironic smile lifting the corners of her mouth. She reached for me and I took her hand, surprised by the strength of her grip. Once she'd taken hold of me, I couldn't break free, no matter how hard I tugged, and the glowing ball was expanding, absorbing me, my vision going pink as my lungs filled with water.

CHAPTER FOURTEEN

I didn't know what time it was. Nor could I bring myself to care. Voices swirled in my head, none of them remotely coherent. Snatches of old popular songs. Lines from movies. A commercial jingle. I shuffled from bedroom to hallway to kitchen, breakfast so habitual that it seemed to make itself: peanut butter on toast, the coffee pot rattling. A flock of geese passed high over the house. The trees might have grown, but none of the houses out the window had changed since I was a boy. Distracted by the birds, I burned my mouth on the steaming coffee. I slammed my mug down and burned my hand. An inward tremor, a backwards tug of the mind, and the sky filled with herons, a small girl in my arms, looking up, her face brimming with wonder. I battered the memory away with my fists and the tremor subsided. The geese had passed out of sight. The house was quiet, the telephone long since disconnected, an empty space in the living room where Dad's old television had once sat. Books lay everywhere, on counters, tables and shelves, many of them propped open at a spot where I'd stopped reading. I left my spilled coffee on the counter, and moved from book to book, reading a page here, a sentence there. Then I found myself on the battered concrete porch in my coat and shoes. The word "mailbox" went through my head. I felt in my pocket for the mail key. It was a windy day and I pulled my collar up before climbing down the stoop. Pain flared in my right knee with every step. A very specific combination of sensory details sent me tumbling back through all the autumns I'd lived in that house: the reds and yellows of the maples, woodsmoke from a chimney, the mild ache of cold air in my lungs. I walked down the rocky path to the front gate with the sticky latch, not at all surprised to see Dad—long dead—on his knees in the front yard, banging pickets onto the fence's frame. The top of his head was pink. He reached into a bucket of nails and a single nail fell to the grass—a nail that would lie there for years, accumulating rust, until it pierced my bare foot, leading to a round of painful tetanus shots. I kicked at the gate and stepped out onto the sidewalk. A hard gust shook the trees and leaves swirled around me. The wind intensified—an atomic wind stripping the land clean, leaving nothing but devastated prairie. Then, as abruptly as it had vanished, the world rebuilt itself: smoke and tepees, wagons and ramshackle cabins; cobblestones, telegraph lines, automobiles, pavement, telephone poles, streetlights. One change led to another, bringing me back to the street as I knew it.

A boy on a bike dodged past me on the sidewalk. The wind blew around my bare ankles. Halfway to the community mailboxes, a car sped by going much too fast and I resisted the urge to throw a rock after it. At the end of the block, I felt my pockets again for the mail key. For a moment, I thought I'd lost it, that I'd come all this way for nothing, then my hand closed around the metal slug and I jammed it into one of the small doors in front of me. The mailboxes made me think of the big wooden advent calendar Dad had lugged out each December, which tipped me into another, more recent memory: a pile of gifts on the floor, a small girl at my feet, gleefully tearing paper. "No," I said, in a firm voice, banishing the image, before looking around to see if anyone had heard me. I opened my mailbox and slid my hand into the narrow cubby, pulling out the usual stack of flyers and bills, surprised to find an envelope with actual handwriting nestled among them. Even if Meredith hadn't identified herself as the sender, I would have recognized her writing from the countless notes she'd left around the house when we were together.

I clutched the envelope to my chest, nearly bending it in half. On the walk home, a high tone sounded in my ears. My lungs forgot when to pull, when to release. My house looked like a neglected church, like a burrow in the mud. I made it to the gate and struggled with the latch. The next-door neighbour came around the side of her house with a rake, her smile fading when she saw me. She said something I couldn't understand, her features pinched in concern. I held up the envelope, meaning sorry no time to talk, and wrestled open the gate. Dad was up on the roof, laying shingles. Dark clouds rolled over the house. Nickel-sized hailstones pounded the grass all around me. I hurried up the stairs, protecting the envelope with my body, threw open the door, and stopped. A little girl was toddling unsteadily towards me.

"Daddy!" she cried.

The structure of the house had changed dramatically, the little foyer opening up into a living area, the upper floor merging with the lower and spreading out. The child nearly fell, wheeled her arms for balance, and kept coming. Her hair had been recently brushed. Her pajamas were clean and covered in cartoon monsters. She took a few last tripping steps and threw herself at me. I thought I wouldn't have the strength to catch her but I did, lifting her up, marvelling at her absence of fear, her unqualified joy at seeing me.

I hugged her close. Christine. Still with me. Still here. She squirmed to be put down, wanting to show me something, but I couldn't let go, couldn't stop hugging her, my arms locked around her little body.

Meredith came out of the kitchen, looking alarmed. "What's wrong?"

I shook my head, unable to speak.

"Felix, what is it? What's happened?"

Christine struggled to get away. "Mommy!"

Meredith took her from me and I staggered back against the wall, then sank to the floor and covered my face with my hands, overwhelmed by the loss of the very people in front of me. Meredith kept saying my name. Eventually, the urgency in her voice got through and I managed to slow my breath and look up.

"I'm sorry," I said.

She was hushing Christine, who looked terrified. "Talk to me," she said. "What's going on?"

I made a vague gesture and realized that I was holding an envelope. Not a letter from Meredith, but a bill from the power company. I held it out to her. "I brought in the mail."

Meredith waited until Christine was down for the evening before approaching me in the TV room. She'd been scheduled to work the night shift and had changed into her scrubs, addressing me in a gentle but firm voice.

"Are you ready to tell me what happened?"

I turned off the television and set the remote aside. "I told you, I was confused."

"Were you seeing things?"

"No."

"Hearing voices?"

"No."

"I need you to be sure about this, Felix."

"I am," I said, still traumatized by the specific way I'd experienced Christine's loss—not as a time-traveller might feel it, with a degree of self-awareness, but as my actual future self, knowing no other reality but that one. I couldn't say exactly how I'd lost her (or why I was back in my old house for that matter), but her absence had been an unchangeable fact of my existence, like an amputated limb.

"This confusion," Meredith said. "Is it still with you now?"

"No." I rubbed my face "I'm fine now, really. I think I might have just forgotten to take my meds."

"What?" she said. "When?"

"Today. And yesterday, maybe."

"Did you check the pill caddy?"

"No."

Meredith hurried out of the room and came back with a long plastic container, looking slightly panicked. "Five days," she said. "You've missed five days, Felix."

"Really?"

She showed me Thursday through Monday, three pills nestled in each little cube. For the second time that evening, I found myself thinking about Dad's old advent calendar: cubbies, compartments, holes...

Meredith shook out Monday's pills and gave them to me. "Here. Take them now."

I hesitated, frowning at the pills in my hand.

"Felix."

"No, you're right. I was just thinking that it's a little late in the day. They might keep me up."

"I'll get you some water."

She went into the kitchen and I stared at the dark television, thinking about Chad Temple's murder, and the oak tree by my old apartment. In both cases, my premonitions had come true. I scoured my mind for specific details from this latest vision, but as my future self, I'd been consciously avoiding any thought of Christine. Meredith came back into the room and handed me a glass of water. It was not a gentle recommendation, but a requirement. I put the pills in my mouth and washed them down.

"Good," Meredith said.

"I'm sorry."

"These things happen. I'll double-check the caddy from now on. I should have been doing it all along."

"Okay."

"How do you feel now?"

"Tired."

She collected her keys and purse and looked at me closely. "Are you going to be all right?"

"Yeah."

She lingered by the front door. "I could stay home, if…"

"It's okay."

"You're positive."

"Yes."

"You'll remember to put her monitor on?"

"I'll remember."

"Call me if you need anything."

"Okay."

"Anything at all."

I kissed her goodbye, applying a few more degrees of pressure than usual to convey a confidence I did not feel.

After she'd pulled out of the driveway, I lay in the dark bedroom, the sensitivity of the baby monitor on high. A low hiss came from the receiver as it registered a sound in the nursery. I listened for a minute, then went down the hall and quietly opened Christine's door. The nursery was dark, a blue halo coming from the nightlight on her dresser. I approached the crib and peered down at her sleeping body: arms stretched out on either side, like she'd died while trying to fly. I watched her chest for the subtle rise and fall of breath. She whimpered in her sleep and I reached down and took her hand in my own. If she was aware of me, she didn't show it, breathing deeply and evenly. I let go of her hand and lay down on the floor beside the crib, watching her face through the bars, trying to guess what dreams were tumbling through her head, whether I was there, and in what guise—loving giant or capricious ogre. Having placed myself between Christine and any conceivable threat, I put my hands behind my head and shut my eyes.

What felt like seconds later, someone turned on the light. I rolled over, groping around on the floor for a weapon. Meredith was standing in the doorway in her scrubs.

"You're back?" I said, groggily.

"It's morning."

"Really?"

"Didn't you hear Christine crying?"

I looked over and saw Christine standing in her crib, her face streaked with tears. Sunlight was leaking around the blackout drapes. Meredith came over and hoisted her out.

"You haven't been in here all night, have you?" she asked me.

I sat up with a groan. "She had a nightmare."

"Oh no." Meredith stroked Christine's face. "Is that right? Did you have a bad dream, honey?" Christine nodded seriously. "Well, everything's all right now. Daddy kept you safe, didn't he?"

She nodded again, though it seemed to me with less certainty. I slowly got to my feet, as Meredith bounced Christine in her arms.

"Silly Daddy," she said, keeping her voice light, while giving me a thoughtful look. "He didn't even have a pillow."

The next night I slept in Christine's room again, with pillows and a blanket, and the night after that. By the end of the week, I'd installed a cheap air mattress on the floor.

"Do you think it's good for her?" Meredith asked over Sunday breakfast. I watched Christine eat a diced-up pancake with her hands, ready to intervene at the first sign of choking.

"It makes me feel better," I said.

"But she's been sleeping so well on her own."

"Well, I'm sorry, but I have concerns."

"What kind of concerns?"

"Things happen."

Meredith sighed. "Nothing's going to happen, Felix."

When we'd first started dating, she'd gone on at length about the children she'd seen in her time in emergency medicine. Kids with drain cleaner in their bellies and missing fingers; mortally injured babies hemorrhaging on gurneys. At the time, she'd maintained that nearly every one of those incidents could have been prevented with a little more adult supervision, but now that Christine was the one at risk, Meredith was strangely cavalier about it all.

"I just think we need to back off a little," she said. "Give her some room to grow."

I put down my utensils, no longer hungry. "In daycare, you mean."

She'd been talking about enrolling Christine in daycare ever since her maternity leave had expired, in spite of my objections. "Well, yes," she said. "Don't you think it would be good for her to be around other kids?"

"She can do that at a playground."

Meredith snorted, then raised a hand. "Sorry."

"What?"

"Nothing. It's just…when have you ever taken her to a playground?"

I glanced over at Christine in her booster seat, wondering how much of this she was taking in. She'd eaten half a pancake and was making swirling patterns in the syrup with her fingers. "Have some eggs, sweetie," I said, and she made a face at me. I'd been cooking more since Meredith had gone back to work: wholesome, balanced meals. I kept the house clean and small objects out of reach. I'd bolted the bookshelves to the walls and stuffed the electrical outlets with protective plugs. I'd rigged the cupboards and doorknobs with childproof devices and installed baby gates at the top and bottom of the stairs. I literally never let Christine out of my sight. No daycare in the world could have kept her half as safe as I could keep her.

"She doesn't need that," I said, as Meredith filled a sippy cup with orange juice.

"What?"

"The juice. It's bad for her teeth."

"It has vitamins."

"It's loaded with sugar."

Meredith put the sippy cup down, looking amused.

"Anyway," I said. "It's too late for daycare. They fill up months in advance."

"That's true. But there's a place not far from the hospital. Olivia—the new intern I've been telling you about?—she knows the owner. She told me they can make room for Christine. They're holding a spot."

"When did you find this out?" I asked, trying to keep my voice casual.

"I don't know. Sometime last week."

"I want deuce," Christine said quietly.

Meredith stroked her head. "I know you want juice, baby."

"Last week? When did you plan on telling me?"

"I'm telling you now. We should at least think about it. They have a really good reputation."

"I want deuce!" Christine said more loudly.

"It sounds expensive," I said, nudging the milk I'd given Christine a bit closer.

"It's actually quite reasonable."

Christine glowered at me. "I. Want. Deuce!"

I grabbed the juice and slammed it onto her tray.

"Settle down," Meredith said.

"It's all she ever drinks," I snapped, wanting to carry Christine to the nursery, close the door, and wall it off with heavy furniture.

Meredith regarded me sternly.

"I'm sorry," I said. "I just have a bad feeling about all this."

"Why?"

Before I could answer, Christine tossed her sippy cup onto the floor. "All done," she announced.

"Are you sure?" I said. "You didn't touch your eggs."

"No like."

"Baby, it's important."

"No like!" She hit her plate with both hands. Scrambled eggs and half-eaten pancakes flew everywhere. I gave her a look and she started to cry. I tried to unstrap her from her booster seat, feeling Meredith watching me.

"Owie!" Christine yelled.

Her leg was caught. I jerked it loose.

"Owiiiiiiie!"

"It's just ketchup," I muttered.

"I want Mama!"

"Daddy's got you," I said.

"I want *mama*!"

Meredith was standing beside me with open hands. I tried to settle Christine for another second, before handing her over, more roughly than I meant to.

"Daddy hurt me," she moaned.

"No," I said. "Daddy was trying to help you."

"Come on." Meredith said, carrying her away from the table. "Let's get you washed up."

They left the room and I heard the tub start running. Soon Christine was happily splashing in the water. I stayed at the table, looking at my half-eaten breakfast, as bells started to ring in the church down the road. I'd never been religious, but felt briefly compelled to obey the call, surrendering to an authoritative stranger who would tell me what to believe, what to do.

"Can you come in here for a second?" Meredith called.

I looked in the bathroom.

"I need to get some towels from the basement. Would you mind sitting with her for a minute?"

"I can get the towels."

"I want you to sit with her," she said, with a meaningful look.

I sighed and changed places with Meredith, regret flooding me as I watched Christine play in the bubbles, a plastic animal in each hand. She lifted one to her mouth.

"No," I said gently, and she gave me a surprised look. "Not in your mouth, sweetie. Dangerous."

She reached for a toy boat on the edge of the tub. I pictured her slipping and hitting her head, her submerged, lifeless body staring up at the ceiling, her fine hair undulating around her face.

"Careful." I reached down to steady her.

She snatched the boat, looking as annoyed as a one-and-a-half-year-old can look.

I noticed Meredith's hair dryer on the counter (unplugged, far from the tub) and tucked it into a drawer. "There," I said. "Daddy's watching. Daddy's not going to let anything bad happen."

A few days later, I took Christine to the playground: hovering beside her, snatching rocks out of her hands, and scanning the grass for sharp objects. "They can hurt you," I explained to Christine. "These things can hurt you." Another group of children showed up, and I subtly discouraged her from playing with them. When a boy with scabbed knees started talking to her, I swooped in to remove her from the interaction, loudly reminding her about a fictional appointment we were late for while she flailed in my arms and screamed, "I wanna stay!"

Back at the house, she immediately began climbing the furniture, using the knobs on her dresser like grips on a climbing wall. I pulled her down and took off the knobs with a screwdriver. At lunch time, I cut her food into smaller and smaller pieces. Still envisioning her choking, I pureed them in the blender.

"No like!" she wailed when I presented her with the mash. "No liiiiiike!"

"It's the same!" I yelled back. "It's exactly the same food!"

When Meredith came back from work, an uneasy calm reigned in the house, me assuring her that everything had gone fine, while Christine sulked, unable to articulate the battles we'd fought throughout the day. That night as I lay beside Christine's crib, watching her sleeping face, I kept returning to the vision I'd had of a future without her. I wanted to believe it had all been in my mind, a projection of my own dark fears, but it just *felt true*. If I was to have any hope of saving her, I needed more information—a time, a place, some broader context—and that was going to mean another trip to the future. I was running out of time. Back-to-school flyers had started showing up in the mailbox. Meredith had purchased a miniature pink backpack and a tiny pair of running shoes. Daycare was happening, no matter how I felt about it, and that meant the potential threats to Christine were about to increase exponentially.

The next morning, I was in the TV room watching cartoons with Christine, when Meredith came out of the bedroom. "Did you take your meds yet?"

"Hm?" I said after a moment, still watching the screen.

"Your meds."

"No. Not yet." I usually took my medication after breakfast, but hadn't made it beyond the couch that morning. I got up and went into the bathroom, leaving Christine with Meredith. The peppy theme song from *Dora the Explorer* bled through the door, making me want to cry. I took down the pill caddy and opened the door for the day. Three pills were waiting for me: a pentagon, a circle and a lozenge. I picked them up and weighed them in my hand for a moment, before tossing them into the toilet, where they sank to the bottom like little capsized boats. Then I flushed them down.

CHAPTER FIFTEEN

It took a few days for something to happen. Every night, Meredith would leave for work just after Christine went to bed and I would check and double-check the doors and windows, then sit on the couch and shut my eyes, straining to detach my mind from my body. When that failed, I tried a more passive approach, breathing slowly and deeply, surrendering to whatever mysterious forces might guide me. Finally, I paced the house, knocking myself about the head in an attempt to physically jar myself out of the present. By the time Meredith came home around dawn, I'd be lucky to have gotten any sleep. Propped at the kitchen table in front of a bright-eyed Christine, I'd jump at the slightest noise: a car door slamming outside, Christine's spoon clanging against her tray.

"God!" I'd snap, before making a conscious effort to modulate my voice. "Sweetie, could you please not do that?"

A malicious gleam would come into Christine's eye and she would bang her tray harder. If Meredith happened to be there, I would shut my eyes and breathe, but if we were alone, I'd shout at Christine, or snatch the spoon from her hand and throw it across the room—a scene that would end with her shrieking in my arms as I tried to console her. By the end of the week, Meredith had begun to look worried, as if she were doing something irresponsible by leaving us alone together, but she kept going to work, always with the same parting question: "Are you sure you're okay? Felix—are you *sure?*"

When she'd gone, I'd peer out the window through a gap in the curtains at a suspicious black car I'd been noticing across the street. In the event that they'd bugged the house, I'd mutter to the empty room, letting them know that I was onto them. One night, after checking all the doors and windows for the fifth time, I secured a long blade from the knife block in the kitchen. I carried the knife to the window and showed it to black car. Then I went into Christine's room and tucked the weapon under my air mattress before going to sleep. On Meredith's next day off, she told me that she was going to take Christine to visit a coworker.

"You'd better not," I said, anxiously watching her put on Christine's shoes.

"Why not?"

"I think she's sick. She was coughing all night."

"Really? She seems fine now. Do you feel okay, sweetheart?"

Christine nodded.

"Maybe I should come with you," I suggested. The offer was so out of character that Meredith stared at me for a long moment.

"No. I think you should stay here and get some rest."

She slid a pair of sunglasses onto Christine's little nose and carried her out the door. If I'd had my own vehicle, I would have jumped in it and tailed them. Instead, I went into the backyard and collapsed on a patio chair. A warm breeze agitated the wind chimes. The hummingbird feeder swayed beside me on its hook. I shut my eyes and watched a truck slam into the passenger side of Meredith's car, in the exact spot where Christine's seat was fastened. I saw the wreckage smoke, then burst into flames, Christine shrieking in the smashed window. I opened my eyes. A hummingbird had dropped from a tree in the neighbour's yard, flitting over to the feeder with quick, jerky movements.

I didn't move, mesmerized by the mossy green of its back, the flare of pink at its throat. Then a hard spasm went through me and I was in a bathtub ringed with grime, surrounded by teal blue tiles, a leaky showerhead dripping at my feet. I looked down the length of my body, from my flabby, grizzled torso to my gnarled toenails. My eyes travelled back up to my arms and lingered on the thick blue channels at my wrists, my penis floating limply between my legs. I had no clear sense of my own identity. My memories seemed to have been emptied from my head, like the contents of a bag shaken over a bed by an indifferent thief. All that remained was this useless old machine and an overwhelming sense of loss. Water dribbled from the showerhead. The house made the occasional ticking noise as it settled on its foundation. Without any forethought, I began to slide down into the filthy water, letting my ears go under first, then my mouth, my nose, and finally my eyes. I lay on my back at the bottom of the tub, counting in my head. At sixty seconds, my body wanted to surface. At two minutes, my lungs started to hurt. I clenched my fists and watched the shimmering ceiling through the water. A third minute passed and pressure filled my head. My belly spasmed, trying to rebreathe the air locked inside it. I'd stopped counting, forcing myself to stay under in spite of the pain. Then I inhaled.

The instant I began to choke, my body forced me up out of the water and back onto the patio. The hummingbird was hovering just inches from my face. I shouted and lunged away from it. My chair toppled. My elbow slammed against the flagstones. The hummingbird retreated and swooped back over the fence. Breathing hard, clutching my arm, I staggered inside and saw Meredith's purse and shoes sitting by the front door. She came out of Christine's room with a finger to her lips.

"You came back," I said.

"Shh," she whispered. "I just got her down...What happened to your arm?"

I looked down, seeing a deep gash on my elbow. "Nothing. It's fine."

"You need to take care of that."

"Did you see that bird out there?"

"What?"

"On the patio. There was a—"

"Hold on, I'll get you a bandage." Meredith disappeared into the bathroom. I looked out the window at the plastic chair, on its side on the patio. The hummingbird hadn't come back. The utter hopelessness I'd felt in what had looked like Dad's old bathtub must have involved Christine, but I still hadn't the faintest idea what was going to happen to her. Needing to see her, I sneaked into the dim nursery and approached the crib on the balls of my feet. I reached down to stroke Christine's hair and her eyes flicked open.

"Hi, sweetheart," I whispered. Before I could say anything else, she started to scream. I tried to pick her up and she batted me away in terror.

A second later, Meredith was at the door. "What happened?"

"I don't know." I said, shouting over Christine. "She woke up like this."

"What were you doing in here?"

"Nothing!"

Christine was sitting up now, shrieking uncontrollably, as if she'd been doused with scalding water. "Baby—" I reached down and she scrambled back against the bars. But when Meredith came over, she allowed herself to be picked up and settled almost instantly.

Meredith looked at me.

"I didn't do anything," I said.

She turned away, swaying and humming to Christine.

"Mer . . "

The volume of humming increased.

"I didn't do anything!"

"I never said you did," she whispered. "Now can you please—"

"You're thinking it. I can see it in your face."

Christine started to cry again. "Go to the other room," Meredith said, firmly.

"I—"

"Can't you see you're scaring her?"

Christine was cowering and keening softly. I wanted to wrench her out of Meredith's arms and shake her, to make her see how much I loved her, how everything I'd done from the moment she'd been born had been for her. I banged my way out of the nursery and marched downstairs to the spare room, where I kept my computer. I felt like throwing the laptop against the wall. Instead, I took a breath, sat down, and, for the first time in years, began to hunt for Jasmine—soothed by the ritual of combing through the endless lists of webcams. Nothing had changed since I'd been away. The coloured rooms hadn't returned. Jasmine remained unfindable. I abandoned my search and googled hummingbird behaviour, still feeling the violent thrumming of wings in my head. From what I read, the birds were notoriously territorial and antisocial, only coming together for the purposes of mating. Although they were known to approach humans, I could find no instances of them actually harming anyone.

I glanced up from the screen. Meredith was in the doorway, watching me.

"Talk to me," she said.

I fidgeted in my chair. "I'm just tired."

"That was beyond tired."

"Is she all right?"

"It took a while, but she's settled."

The article I'd been reading showed two hummingbirds engaged in aerial combat. I closed the laptop and set it aside. "I'm sorry."

"You need to talk to Dr. Patel."

"Why?"

"*Why?* Felix—"

"I can handle this," I insisted. "It's not that big of a deal."

"It's a very big deal. This anger of yours... You're not having any bad thoughts, are you?"

"Absolutely not."

"And the delusions?"

"None."

"You've been taking your medication."

"Of course."

"I really think—"

"One more chance," I said. "That's all I'm asking. If I lose my temper again, I'll go to Dr. Patel. I swear to God."

Meredith ran her hands through her hair, clearly overwhelmed. "You'll have to move out of her room," she said. "It's not helpful."

"You mean you don't trust me."

"Don't start that again."

"I would never hurt Christine," I said, growing emotional.

Meredith sighed, looking as exhausted as I felt. "This is non-negotiable, Felix. She has to start sleeping on her own."

That night, I slept on the couch in the TV room, playing with the smartphone Meredith had brought home so we could keep in touch while she was at work. Beyond text messaging, I hadn't thought I'd have much use for the device, but once I'd gotten used to the smaller screen, it was rarely out of my hand. I revisited all the old sites I'd haunted as a bachelor, watching women on webcams, not quite certain if what I was doing was wrong. By the fourth night, I'd mastered the app store and had downloaded an adult chat application, using the name Father Time Traveller (this time fairly sure I was doing something wrong). Within two minutes, a girl called Sad Jazz gave me a digital nudge.

wanna chat?

Her profile said she was twenty-eight years old with an athletic build, green eyes, and red hair. I quietly checked on Christine, before going back to the couch and typing, *Sure. Where are you from?*

The house was dark, my smartphone glowing. Her response came a split second later: *hollywood.*

My heart quickened at the word, the lowercase H. *Really?*

yup. how about you?

I considered for a moment. *Hollywood.*

no way.

It's true.

small world.

I could feel her grinning on the other end, knowing as well as I did that neither one of us was in Hollywood.

So, I wrote back, *what are you up to tonight?*

waiting.

What for?

the drugs to kick in.

Recreational?

prescription.

Psychiatric?

yahtzee.

What's your diagnosis?

Bipolar…yourself?

Schizoid tendencies.

Impressive…are you married?

Common-law, I confessed. *You?*

yes, indeed.

Where's your significant other?

out with friends…yours?

Night shift.

ah.

So...I fondled myself idly through my sweatpants. Do you want to know what I look like?
not really.
I frowned at my screen.
nothing personal. it's just that we're never going to meet.
But we live so close, I reminded her.
hahaha. riiiight.
Neither of us said anything for a minute.
time traveller, she finally wrote.
Yes?
this is the schizoid part.
Maybe.
where do you go?
Lately? To the future.
and what does the future hold?
Nothing good.
too bad...
I'm starting to wonder if I can change things. Make them better.
how?
I'm working on that.
After a long pause, she wrote: *maybe I can help.*
With what?
improving your future.
What did you have in mind?
i have a few ideas...
I grinned, increasingly sure that Jazz and Jasmine were one and the same person. *Can I ask you something?*
shoot.
Do I know you?
now that's a question.
And what's the answer?
A weighty silence.
i think we might have met before...
Really?

stranger things have happened.

I hadn't used the camera on my smartphone for much yet, other than taking a few snapshots of Christine. Now I turned on the overhead light and took a shot of my body from the waist down—sweatpants and socks, stretched out across the couch. I touched an icon of a camera and the photo appeared in the chat stream.

Look familiar? I typed.

maybe, she wrote back. *show me more.*

» » »

Cruel sunlight poured in through the window above the sink. Hunched in my chair, I watched Christine shovel sugar-free cereal into her mouth while Meredith flicked through a fashion magazine on the other side of the table. I felt uncomfortable manipulating the objects in front of me—my spoon, my cup. My phone made a harsh chirping noise in my pocket and I jumped, then pulled it out. The chat application I'd been using had installed push notifications on my phone without my being aware of it. A new message from Jazz filled half the screen: *good morning.*

Meredith raised her eyebrows.

"Wrong number," I muttered, turning off the ringer and tucking the phone back into my pocket.

"Text?"

I nodded.

"You should let them know."

"They'll figure it out."

My phone buzzed against my thigh as another notification arrived. I lifted my cup, dismayed to find it empty. The coffee machine seemed very far away. My phone buzzed again. I wondered if Meredith could hear it across the table.

"How was your night?" I asked.

"Long," she said, eyes on her magazine.

"What about you?" I ruffled Christine's hair. "How did you sleep, baby girl?"

She glowered at me. "I want deuce."

"I'll get it in a second, honey."

As my phone vibrated yet again, a grinning, mask-like face suddenly appeared in the kitchen window. "Jesus!" I shouted, as the face ducked out of sight.

"What is it?" Meredith said.

"Someone's out there." I hurried to the window.

Meredith came up behind me. "I don't see anyone."

It was true. The yard was empty. It didn't seem possible that they could have escaped so quickly. A wave of dizziness hit me and I gripped the counter to keep from falling over.

"Are you all right?" Meredith asked.

"What?" I said, having trouble focusing on her. "Yeah. I'm just tired." I looked out the window again. "I was sure..."

"Have you taken your meds?"

"Hm? No, not yet." My phone buzzed and I put my hand over my pocket, this time sure Meredith had heard. "I'll go take them now," I said. "Before I forget."

On my way through the TV room, I checked the picture window for the idling black car, finding it just where I'd expected. "Fuck off," I hissed to whoever might be listening. Back in the kitchen, I could hear Meredith talking to Christine about daycare.

"Eight more sleeps, honey..."

I locked myself in the bathroom and pulled out my phone, reading the four messages Jazz had sent.

8:53 - hey tiger.

8:55 - are you there?

8:57 - babe?

8:58 - helloooo.

Bad time, I quickly typed back.

She responded instantly. *why? what's up?*

I frowned at the phone. Alone in the dark, I'd been convinced that I'd found Jasmine again. But Jasmine would never have been so needy, so desperate to get in touch. The woman (assuming she *was* a woman) was an utter stranger. I didn't owe her a thing. I closed the chat window and dragged the program to the garbage can at the top of my screen. The phone made a little vacuum noise as it sucked the application away. I returned the phone to my pocket, then took out my pills for the day and flushed them down the toilet before going back out to the kitchen. The table was empty, the dishes cleared away.

"Mer?"

I went through the entire main level, then checked the basement and jogged back upstairs. Their shoes were gone. The driveway was empty. I hauled out my phone and stopped, noting that the date on my home screen had changed. If it was accurate, I'd just lost three days. My phone vibrated. I touched the home button and found the application I'd just deleted, reinstalled, with a new message waiting. I opened the chat window, confronted by the last few messages of an ongoing exchange:

are they gone?

Just now.

does she suspect?

I don't know, maybe.

do we care?

Just a second.

That was the last thing I'd written. The message Jazz had sent a moment ago read: *still there, babe?*

I shut the app and dragged it up to the garbage. An instant after it disappeared, it occurred to me that I should have read the rest of the conversation. I had no idea how long we'd been talking, what we'd said, how much I'd revealed. Something banged against the living room window and I flinched, then looked out and found a hummingbird hovering close to the glass. I snapped the curtains shut and sent Meredith a text: *Where are you?*

I paced to the kitchen, where I saw not one but several hummingbirds darting around the backyard feeder. I shut the kitchen blinds and sent Meredith a second, more urgent text. *Write me as soon as you get this.* Over the next hour, I sent text after text, while small shadows flitted across the drawn curtains. When I finally worked up the nerve to look outside again, the air was filled with whirring hummingbirds. Hardly able to dial, I called Meredith's number and left what I hoped sounded like a relatively normal message. "Hey, it's me. Did you get my texts? There's a...situation here. Call me." I hung up and immediately phoned again. Before long, I'd filled up her machine, and was forced to switch back to texts—keeping things vague, not mentioning the birds. There were thousands of them now, roiling in the windows like theoretical particles. I crawled into bed and pulled the covers over my head, having all but convinced myself that I was never going to see Meredith or Christine again, until I heard the distinctive sound of an engine in the driveway. I looked out and saw Meredith walking around the car to collect Christine. The hummingbirds had vanished.

Where were you?" I demanded, charging out to meet them in my bare feet.

Meredith hoisted Christine out of her car seat, looking confused. "At the rec centre."

"Oh." I'd forgotten that Christine had a music class every Sunday morning. "Well, did you get my messages?"

"No, my phone was off."

"Daddy!" Christine chirped.

Meredith swerved around me with Christine in her arms. "Come on, honey. Let's give you a bum change."

I followed them into the house, where Meredith laid Christine on the change table in the nursery. I hovered behind her. "So...you were at Toddler Tunes?"

"Of course."

"How'd it go?"

"Fine."

I peered over Meredith's shoulder. "Did you have fun at music class, pumpkin?"

Meredith shot me an annoyed look. "Do you mind?"

"What?"

"You're crowding me."

I stepped back and she positioned herself firmly between me and Christine, taking what felt like forever to put on a new diaper.

"There we go," she said, picking Christine up. "Come on, let's get you a snack." She carried Christine past me into the kitchen and started going through cupboards. "When did you say their flight was coming?" she asked me.

"Um..."

"Never mind, here it is." Meredith pulled a yellow sticky note off the fridge. "Five o'clock. That gives us, what? Four hours?" She handed Christine a teething biscuit and shifted her from one hip to the other, holding her like she never intended to put her down. "They're bound to be hungry when they get here. We should pick up some snacks. What do they like to eat?"

"I—I'm not sure," I stammered, unable to imagine who "they" might be, or why I'd know anything about their dietary habits. Up in Meredith's arms, Christine had started to squirm. "She wants down," I said.

"What?"

"Christine. She wants down."

Meredith reluctantly set her on the floor. "Go play nice in your room, okay?"

"Kay." Christine toddled out of the kitchen.

"Daddy will be there in a minute!" I called after her.

"Oh, no you won't," Meredith said. "I need you to set up the spare room downstairs."

I wasn't sure what I found more troubling, the revelation that someone was actually going to be staying with us, or the tone Meredith was taking with me, as if I were a disobedient child. I had no choice but to pretend it was all perfectly normal. If she knew I'd been missing time again, I would find myself back at the psychiatric unit that very afternoon. I peered into Christine's room on my way to the basement and found her sitting on the floor, whispering into the ear of a plush doll.

"What's the secret?" I asked, smiling at her.

She jumped and started to cry. Meredith was in the room in an instant. "What happened?"

"Nothing." I held up my hands.

"Daddy scare me!"

"Honey, I didn't mean to scare you. I was just saying hello."

Meredith gave me an exasperated look and I stormed out of the room, not bothering to defend myself, going downstairs and slamming both baby gates behind me. My phone buzzed. I took it out and looked at it. The dating app was back. "Jesus Christ!" I shouted and dragged it up to the trash with a vicious swipe of the finger. I shut my eyes and took a breath, before continuing on to the spare room. Just as I was about to open the door, it swung open of its own accord and I found myself facing a tall, well-tanned man with a bleached goatee. "Ho! Gave me a jump there! How you going, Felix?" The man chuckled, then looked concerned. "Say, are you all right, mate?"

Judging from his accent and the open suitcase on the bed, I assumed this could only be my sister's husband, a man I'd never met. "I'm fine," I said. "I'm sorry. Is Eileen here?"

"She's upstairs with the boys, isn't she?"

"Right. I just came down to...check on something."

"Oh, all right." He gave me an affable smile.

I turned back to the stairs and banged my shin on the open baby gate. "Fuck!" I shouted, aware that Eileen's husband was watching me. My phone buzzed and I looked at it. Once again, the dating app was back, with another text from Jazz.

family still there?

With mounting panic, I swept the app into the garbage and resumed climbing. Upstairs, the blinds were wide open, sunlight flooding the house. Meredith was in the kitchen, wearing the same dress she'd worn on our first date. "Did you find the camera?" she asked, her face shining, as if she'd had a couple of drinks.

"I...No."

"Well, I'll have a look for it later." She held out a glass of red wine. "Can you bring this to your sister?"

Christine's high-pitched laughter rang out deeper in the house. I took the glass and rounded the corner to find my sister—older and thinner than I remembered her—in an armchair in the TV room. Across from her, two boys in their early teens sat on the couch, flanking Christine, who was standing unsteadily on the middle cushion.

She rocked forwards.

"No!" I lunged to catch her, but she made a small correction and plopped down in the taller boy's lap. I'd spilled Eileen's wine all over the floor. "Sorry," I said, battered by all these new faces. "She was about to—"

Christine took two big moon steps across the couch. "Hey!" I shouted, intercepting her. "The couch is for sitting! Not bouncing!"

The boys exchanged a wary look. They looked like gangly, pimpled versions of the Kiwi in the basement.

"Why don't you do something quiet," I said, carrying Christine over to a spot on the floor, aware that I was making a spectacle of myself. "Like colouring."

Christine arched her back. "Lemme go!"

"Honey..." I said, desperately.

"She's fine," Eileen assured me. "The boys won't let her fall."

I ignored her, looking for crayons as Christine shrieked and pounded her heels on the hardwood.

"Everything all right?" Meredith asked, coming out of the kitchen.

"What does it look like?" I snapped.

I didn't care if they were family, I wanted these people out of my house. Eileen cleared her throat. "Do you have any paper towels, Meredith?"

"I'll get them," I muttered, unable to stop Christine from racing back over to the couch.

I ran into Eileen's husband again in the kitchen, my once-peaceful sanctuary transformed into a sinister unpredictable funhouse—unpleasant surprises lurking around every corner. He greeted me with a broad smile.

"I'm getting paper towels," I said, unnecessarily.

"Someone have an accident?"

I opened and closed cupboards, ignoring the roll of paper towels on the counter. Eileen's husband made a clicking noise in the side of his mouth and went off to join the others in the TV room. When he'd gone, I frowned at one of Christine's finger paintings on the fridge, trying to remember his name. Peter. His name was Peter. I congratulated myself on remembering that much, although I still had no idea what they were doing there. As I reached for the roll of paper towels, my smartphone vibrated in my pocket, repeatedly this time, as from an incoming call. I took it out and the display showed an unknown number. I stuffed the phone back in my pocket. The moment it stopped vibrating, the landline began to ring.

I stared at the cordless on the counter.

"Are you getting that?" Meredith called from the TV room.

I picked it up and cautiously touched the talk button.

"Hello?" I said in soft voice.

No one answered.

"Hello?" I repeated, a little louder.

I could hear a television playing on the other end. Someone inhaled, about to speak. I quickly pressed the end button. Out in the living room, Meredith laughed at something Peter was saying. The landline rang again. I picked up just long enough to hang up on the caller, then left the phone off the hook and tucked the cordless into a drawer. "Who keeps calling?" Meredith asked, as I came out of the kitchen.

"No one."

I stopped in front of the spilled drink. I'd forgotten paper towels. As I went back to collect them, my smartphone vibrated in my pocket. I ignored it and cleaned up the mess, before sitting down in a chair apart from the main group. Meredith and Eileen pulled their chairs together, talking in low voices, as Christine bounced from one boy to the other on the couch. Peter glanced my way, trying to catch my eye.

"So," he finally said. "Working on a new book?"

I shook my head. "No."

"Writer's block, eh?" he said knowingly. I let the comment pass. My cellphone rumbled against my thigh. Peter leaned back to watch Christine. "She's adorable," he said, determined to draw me into conversation. I responded with a noncommittal grunt, almost hoping she'd fall and hurt herself so that everyone in the room would see how right I'd been, but as close as she came to the edge, she never went over.

By the end of the night, I'd stopped wondering why Eileen and her family had come, focused instead on the problem of making them leave. The phones had finally quit ringing. My anxiety gave way to exhaustion. Meredith brought in pizza and the boys ate an incredible amount, while Peter got steadily drunker—and louder—regaling me with rambling stories from his youth. When he finally swayed off to bed, Meredith took Christine into the nursery, leaving Eileen and me alone in the living room. Like Peter, my sister had been drinking throughout the night, but unlike him, she seemed relatively sober.

"So," she said. "How is everything?"

"Oh...fine."

"Really?"

"Yes. Why wouldn't it be?"

She shrugged and looked down at her glass. "It looks like you've got a good thing going here. Meredith seems like a nice person."

"She's a saint," I said.

"You're lucky to have found her."

"I'm aware of that."

She looked at me closely, then sat back and sighed. "So how do you want to do this?"

"I'm sorry?"

"The house. How do you want to do it?"

"Which house?"

"Dad's house."

"What about it?"

Meredith laughed. "Jesus, Felix. We talked about this just a few days ago. Why do you think I'm here?"

"I..."

"You agreed that it was time to sell."

"Right." I had no recollection of saying that or anything else to Eileen in the recent past. She set her drink down and leaned towards me.

"Don't tell me you're having second thoughts."

"Well..." Now that she mentioned it, giving up the house felt like a terrible idea.

"The market's hot right now. We'll never get a better price."

I nodded. "Yeah, I get that. It's just...Doesn't it still feel like home to you?"

"No," she said, without hesitation. "It's just an old building filled with bad memories. My home's in Perth, with Peter and the boys. I was never happy in that house, Felix. With Dad moping around and the constant drinking..." She raised her wine glass to acknowledge the irony of the statement. "I'm a pleasant drunk. Dad was a miserable drunk. I don't think he ever forgave himself for what happened to Mom."

"What do you mean?"

"Well, he felt responsible, didn't he? Like he should have done something to protect her."

"From the cancer?" I asked, confused.

Eileen sat back and frowned. "You mean he never told you?"

A low droning noise started up somewhere nearby, as if one of the hummingbirds had found its way into the house.

Eileen shook her head. "I thought that considering all the problems you'd had, he'd have at least..." She trailed off. "Mom never had cancer, Felix. That was just a story Dad told us as kids."

I rubbed at my right ear. "I don't understand."

"She was mentally ill."

I waved at the air beside my head, feeling the hummingbird whirring closer.

"I'm not sure that she ever got a diagnosis," Eileen continued. "But she had major problems. One day Dad came home from work and found us outside, alone in the snow. Mom was inside, having a bath. It wasn't the first time something like that happened. She went places in her head. She forgot about us."

"Dad told you this."

"Yeah."

"But if she didn't have cancer, how did she..."

"She killed herself."

I stared at her and she gave me a tight smile.

"Sorry. I know it's a lot to take in."

I continued to stare at her, no longer sure who I was talking to.

She shifted in her chair. "Felix, I have a confession to make. I'm not just here about the house. You know how I told you on the phone that I tracked you down online? Well, that wasn't exactly true. Meredith contacted me. She's been concerned about you. I mean, the house had been on my mind, but when Meredith told me what was happening...Anyway, Peter has a friend at Qantas. He was able to get us reasonable fare under the circumstances."

I nodded. "Interesting."

The hummingbird buzzed in my head, tunneling towards my brain. My vision darkened at the edges. I wondered how long they'd been talking behind my back, what they were planning to do. Eileen was still talking, but I was having trouble hearing her.

"*They're going to take her away.*"

The words cut through all the noise. A man's clear voice coming from directly behind me. I jerked around in my seat, finding no one there.

"What is it?" Eileen asked.

"Nothing," I said quickly. "I'm sorry, what were you saying?"

"That medication can lose its effectiveness over time. It's possible that you just need to increase the dose a little. I find that with my thyroid meds..."

My phone, which had fallen silent for the evening, woke up and buzzed in my pocket, not with the usual drawn out rings, but with short, regular pulses, like a drumbeat. My vision continued to narrow. I felt as if I'd been holding my breath for a very long time. I exhaled, letting the air leak from my lungs. Then the room went dark.

At first, I thought the power had gone out, but the bathroom light was still on, and the chair Eileen had been sitting in a moment before was empty. I looked at my phone. Three in the morning. I got up and headed for the nursery. Christine appeared to be in her crib, but even up close, with the help of her nightlight, I couldn't be sure that it was actually her. I turned on the overhead light. She didn't move. Her skin looked waxy, like an eerily realistic doll. I reached down to give her a gentle shake.

"Pumpkin," I said. "Wake up."

Her eyes opened halfway. A live girl then, but was it really her? Something didn't feel right. She closed her eyes again and I shook her harder, raising my voice. "Wake up, honey. Can you hear me? Can you wake up for Daddy now?" A thump came from behind me and I whirled to find Meredith in the room in her nightgown. She spoke to me slowly, in what sounded like a foreign language. I shook my head, standing between her and Christine.

"No," I said. "You can't have her."

She moved towards the crib and I caught her by the arms and powered her back out of the room. I shoved her to the floor, then slammed the door and locked it. A high-pitched yowl came through the closed door. The knob rattled. I went back to the crib, where Christine had fully woken and was watching me with fear in her eyes.

"We have to go now," I said, gently picking her up. "We don't have much time."

Meredith pounded at the door, her voice joined by others—a chorus of screeches and growls. I tried to open the window, but found that it had been painted shut. I swore and looked around for something to break the glass.

"Felix!"

The door banged open. Meredith, Eileen, and Peter all burst into the room—Peter in the lead, a switchblade glinting in his hand, my sister clutching a pistol. My phone buzzed against my thigh. "Leave me alone!" I shouted at my leg. Then, to the people in the doorway: "Get back!"

Eileen lifted the gun to her ear, talking to it in a frantic voice. Peter advanced, showing me his empty palms. I circled the crib, realizing that if I was going to get out of there, I was going to have to go through them. "Okay," I muttered, hugging Christine to my chest and lowering my centre of gravity. "Daddy's got you," I whispered in her ear. "Everything's going to be all right. Just close your eyes...Here we go."

CHAPTER SIXTEEN

"How do I know," I asked Dr. Patel, "that none of it's real?"

He shrugged philosophically. The blinds behind his desk were open, presenting a view of a sky so pale it was almost white. "There's an element of trust here," he said. "One might even call it faith. What I *can* tell you is that if we were to put you in an MRI machine, we could see the overactive and underactive parts of your brain. On medication, we could observe a physical change corresponding to the psychological one. But I have a feeling that's not the answer you're looking for."

"No," I admitted.

"What would you rather I'd said?"

"That it's possible I've seen the future."

Patel's office was painted in warm, neutral tones, the walls devoid of pictures. He had a box of tissues on his desk and a small electronic tablet that he consulted from time to time. Otherwise, he made his notes by hand on paper. From the fidgety motion of his pen, he seemed to be drawing at the moment, rather than writing.

"There's a phrase," he said, without looking up from his paper. "I'm sure you've heard it. *A willing suspension of disbelief.* It's how we engage with any fantastic story. We turn off the skeptical part of our minds that's telling us something doesn't make sense. Men can't fly. Corpses can't walk. People are never that articulate or that beautiful in real life. For you, the story is the world—a world governed by rules that nearly everyone agrees to abide by. If you want to engage with that world, or anyone in it, you're going to have to ignore the small voice in the back of your head telling you that *your* world is different. You're going to have to suspend your disbelief...I can't force you to take your medication, Felix. But if you want to go back to your family—"

"It's too late for that," I said.

He stopped drawing and looked at me. "How do you know?"

"Meredith could never forgive me."

"Has she told you that?"

"Not in so many words."

One corner of his mouth lifted. "Is it possible that you're the one who can't forgive yourself?"

I looked at my hands.

"And your daughter?" he asked.

"I'm doing this for her," I said, repeating something I'd been telling myself for months.

"Do you think she sees it that way?"

"It doesn't matter how she sees it."

"Doesn't it?"

"If you had children..."

"What makes you think I don't?"

I looked up in surprise, unable to imagine him as a father, or having any existence at all outside the walls of the hospital. "Well, if one of your kids was dying," I said, "wouldn't you do anything you could to save them? Even if it meant giving them up?"

"If, God forbid, I had a terminally ill child, I would cherish whatever time we had left."

I grunted, doubting that he even had kids.

He tapped his pen on his desk. "When did you last see your daughter, Felix?"

"I don't know. It must be...three months now."

"Don't you want to see her?"

"Of course I do."

"There can be no visitation until you're properly medicated. It was a condition of your release. You understand that, don't you?"

I nodded grimly, annoyed by his use of passive language, as if he hadn't been the one to impose the condition in the first place.

He returned to his notepad, tilting his pen at a deep angle, apparently shading.

"Do you feel that you're a good father, Felix?"

I'd asked myself that question often enough to have a prompt answer. "Yes, I do."

"Why?"

"A good father protects their children."

"Is that what you feel you're doing by ignoring my recommendations? Protecting your daughter?"

"Yes, it is."

"I'm sorry to hear that."

He glanced at his watch. Our session was coming to an end. The rest of his questions were predictable. Did I feel that someone in particular was threatening Christine? Was I having suicidal thoughts? Had I been behaving erratically? Hallucinating?

I denied everything, having learned to answer in absolutes, leaving no room for interpretation. I wanted to see the sketch Patel had been working on, but he tore it off his pad and slipped it into my file, then gave me a placid smile.

"Well..." I said, beginning to get up.

"How do you feel about Meredith?" he asked, not quite finished with me after all.

I sat back down, choosing my words carefully. "I...understand her perspective."

"Which is?"

"She's doing what she thinks is best for Christine."

"And for you."

I shrugged, unwilling to make that concession.

He gave me another half-smile. "Are you still at the same motel?"

"For the moment."

"Be sure to let us know if anything changes."

His desire to keep me there broke the surface of his gaze, like the dorsal fin of a shark. For a moment I worried there were orderlies outside the door, waiting to wrestle me to the ground. "So…" I said.

Patel's half-smile went away. "We'll see you next Thursday, Felix."

» » »

A special discomfort below alerted me to the fact that I'd recently shat myself. Partially reclined, pinned to the bed by a crisp blue sheet, I stared at whatever happened to be in front of me. White walls. White ceiling. A buzzing white tube overhead. I coughed and pain spasmed through my body. I waited for the spell to pass. Somewhere in the room, a game show was playing at low volume. A studio audience cheered. My mouth was dry, my throat on fire. The quality of light on my left suggested the presence of a window, but when I strained my eyes in that direction, I could detect only the vaguest shimmer of blue. After an unknowable amount of time, I heard someone come into the room, a woman I couldn't name, but associated with terrible things.

"Smell that?" she said to someone else. "Come on. Let's flip him over."

Before I could protest, two pairs of rough hands gripped me without warning and rolled me onto my side. I tried to scream, but the sound that left my mouth was barely a moan. I was facing the window now, my back exposed. As they pried the soiled diaper from my body, I caught a brief image of Christine on the change table. Her sweet, trusting face as I held her ankles with one hand and wiped with the other, as gently as I could.

"God," the woman said. "Hold this. It's everywhere."

"This" apparently referred to my leg. New hands took hold of my thigh. I arched and scream-moaned again, as they scoured my anus with what felt like an acid-soaked rag. A bird flashed past the window. A fleeting streak of darkness. Dad stepped into my line of vision and took a thermometer from my mouth.

"Jesus. You're burning up."

"Sorry," I murmured.

"Don't be stupid." He smoothed my hair back from my forehead, then retreated from the bed.

"Come back," I whispered.

I'd been fitted with a clean diaper. Hands wedged under me and prepared to return me to a supine position. "Stop," I muttered, but an agonizing jerk forced me back to where I'd started. Through spots of pain, Meredith swam into view, hovering over me, naked and smiling. I stared at her in astonishment, tears slipping down my face. My bedding was hastily rearranged, the sheet jerked up to my chest. Then, without having said a word to me, my tormentors left the room.

Darkness spread across the ceiling. After a moment, I could make out plush blackout drapes and a blank flat screen television at my feet. I lifted my head without pain. The clock on the motel nightstand read 10:37 a.m. I sat up and swung my legs off the bed, stunned by the ease of motion. I'd never travelled so far into the future before. Contrary to what I'd been telling Dr. Patel, I'd been jumping around in time ever since he'd discharged me, often finding myself alone in Dad's old house, always avoiding any conscious thought of Christine. Now that I knew what lay beyond that time, I felt compelled to get moving while I was still physically able. I jumped out of bed and quickly showered and dressed, then grabbed my phone and wallet and stepped out onto the motel parking lot. Two doors down, a young family was in the process of loading up their minivan—on an early Christmas holiday, I assumed. In the back of the vehicle, I could see a small girl strapped into her car seat like a fighter pilot, staring at a flickering handheld device, while her father tried to puzzle their luggage into place behind her.

A woman came out and talked to the man. They looked like models from a catalogue, attractive and sportily dressed, with perfect hair. They didn't look at me, but I could tell by the stiffness of their exchange that they were aware of me watching them. I wanted to say something, to show them that I was harmless, that I too had a daughter, that we were essentially the same. But as they carried on packing their things and talking in falsely bright voices, I found myself hating them, wishing their trip would end in disaster.

The man closed the hatch and gave me an alpha male stare. I pulled out my phone and frowned at the blank display, as if I'd just gotten an important text. Then I put my head down and walked off through the parking lot to the bus stop. The minivan rolled past a minute later, hardly making a sound, the man and his wife both wearing sunglasses and looking straight ahead, their daughter barely visible in the darkened back window. I shaded my eyes against the late morning sun. After days of cold, relentless showers, the clouds had finally cleared off, and while the air remained cool, the city looked vibrant and invigorated. I consulted the timetable on the pole in front of me and let several buses pass before climbing on a packed double-decker, requesting a transfer from the driver. Warehouses and old brick buildings slid past until we came to a central transportation hub, where I switched buses and headed east, towards the university. At the student union building, I got off and wandered around the campus, unshaven, wearing clothes that hadn't been washed in weeks. A low, sinister-looking building had been erected across from the library since I'd last been there. I stopped to read the sign on the lawn:

INTERFAITH CHAPEL.
OPEN 9AM TO 6PM.
ALL WELCOME.

The front doors were tinted, obscuring the interior of the building. I pictured faiths of all stripes, holding hands and singing non-specific hymns to the beat of a tambourine. I thought about going inside.

"Felix?"

I turned to find a smiling, well-dressed Asian man with a briefcase. "I thought it was you!" Wariness entered his face as he registered the finer details of my appearance, from my oversized second-hand parka to my falling-apart shoes. "Wow. It's been a long time." He chuckled. "You don't remember me, do you."

"Um..."

"Henry Thu," he said. "We were roommates in first year."

"Oh...right."

"So what have you been doing all this time?"

I shrugged and muttered something that had the cadence of speech but no actual meaning. He nodded seriously, as if I'd strung together a coherent sentence. "Okay, okay...Well, I've been teaching here for a few years now. Married. Two kids. Both in school..." His eyes slid over to the interfaith chapel then came back to me. "So you've been well?"

I nodded automatically, wondering if he thought of us as friends.

"That's good." He looked at his watch and made a face. "Geez, I should really get going. I've got a class in ten minutes. But it was great seeing you again. Take care of yourself, okay?"

"Okay," I said, blinking back tears.

Henry walked off briskly, not looking back, our old dormitory tower just visible beyond the sprawl of classroom buildings. I began to follow him, thinking I'd handled the exchange all wrong, but I lost sight of him in a crowd of chatting students and found myself standing by one of the roads that looped through the campus. Another bus came along and I climbed on, using my transfer to get downtown, where I wandered past my first apartment, then walked down to Zoe's high-rise and Kim's place above the Chinese grocer, forcing myself to make eye contact with everyone I saw, willing them to grab hold of me and stop my gathering momentum. My transfer had expired by this time and I stopped in a convenience store to make change for bus fare. The old man behind the counter insisted I buy something first and I grabbed a cheap pair of sunglasses and a ball cap from a clearance bin, putting them on the instant I walked out the door. Everything was coming together. The bus I'd been thinking about all day rolled up, as if summoned. I was the only passenger, riding towards a part of the city I'd passed through many times before but never stopped in. All the usual landmarks streamed by, my breathing slowing as we came in sight of a rundown church with a hand-painted sign above the door: SUNNYVIEW DAYCARE.

I reached for the wire above the window and pulled. The bus rolled to a stop directly in front of the church. I climbed off, sunglasses and hat on. Across the street, a man in a panel van spoke into his wrist. A sniper scope glinted from a neighbouring rooftop. I found the main entrance around the side of the building and hauled open a heavy wooden door. In the dim, empty foyer, a sign directed me down a flight of stairs to a long hallway lined with tiny shoes and colourful knapsacks on hooks. I took off my sunglasses, slowing at what appeared to be Christine's bag, hung beside a closed door, behind which cheerful music was playing. Feeling surprisingly calm, I opened the door and stepped into a large and noisy space with a low ceiling and a scuffed parquet floor. I scanned the room, counting two adults, both women, along with fifteen or so kids, clustered around different play areas.

The taller of the women saw me and came over with a friendly but guarded smile.

"Can I help you?"

I started to answer and stopped, having spotted Christine on the far side of the room, in pigtails and an orange jumper. She and two other little girls were working on a block fortress with high walls and turrets. I plotted my course through the toys and crafting supplies to her play area and then over to the door at the back of the room, behind which I assumed I would find a second staircase. There was no time for explanations. I would grab her and run. The women would chase me, but I would be faster, and I doubted that they'd engage me physically. After all, Christine wasn't their child. The men surveilling the church might present more of a challenge, but I'd elude them somehow, and when we finally reached a quiet spot, I'd sit Christine down and tell her what was happening. The ladies at the daycare weren't bad people, I'd explain, but they didn't know how protect her. Not like I could protect her. She might not realize it, but she was in terrible danger, and I was the only person in the whole world who could keep her safe. I pictured her serious little face taking this all in, then tilting up to ask an obvious question: *Where's Mommy?*

The entire right side of my head was vibrating. I put my hand up to quiet it. I still hadn't spoken to the tall woman, who was looking increasingly worried.

Across the room, Christine's dark eyes locked onto my face. Having been separated for so long, I expected her to shout *Daddy!* then rush over and leap into my arms. But she stayed where she was, watching me, as one watches a line of thunderheads on the horizon. The quietness of that transition, from innocent play to dread, brought with it a sudden and terrible revelation.

I was the threat. These women were here to protect Christine from *me*.

"Cathy," the tall woman said sharply, not taking her eyes off me, and I wondered if she might not put up a fight after all.

The other woman, who'd been crouched beside a little boy in a paint smock, got to her feet.

I raised my hands and backed towards the door.

"It's all right," I said. "I'm leaving."

Neither of the women responded, an inaudible note of alarm passing from them to the children, who, along with Christine, had begun to watch me. The tall woman reached for a smartphone on a desk. I wanted to say something to Christine, to tell her that I loved her, that I was sorry, but she wouldn't have heard. I was in another time, another place, the distance between us unbridgeable. The woman punched at her phone. I hurried out of the room, jogging down the hall, taking the stairs up to the foyer by twos. Out on the street, everything was moving too fast, sunlight crashing off every reflective surface. The tall woman appeared in the doorway behind me, the phone at her ear. I jammed on my sunglasses and ran for the bus stop. The panel van was gone, the sniper nowhere to be seen. A bus rumbled up and I jumped on, flinging a handful of change into the coin box. As the bus pulled into traffic, I stayed on my feet, averting my eyes from the other passengers, waiting for the wail of sirens to come. No squad car pulled us over. No SWAT team stormed the bus.

Eventually, I grabbed a schedule from a pouch on the wall and followed the route of whatever bus I was riding to its end point. The airport. I thought about the things I'd left behind at the hotel. Nothing essential. Nothing that couldn't be replaced. A chime sounded and a young man climbed off, leaving an empty seat near the back of the bus. I steadied myself against the sway of the vehicle and made my way down to the spot he'd vacated, settling in for the ride.

CHAPTER SEVENTEEN

The yard was thick with weeds. A realtor's sign lay on its side in the grass, where a storm or vandals had knocked it. I climbed out of the taxi and stood on the sidewalk before a property that I now owned. Eileen had let me buy her out. We hadn't had any interest since we'd listed it anyway, the market having cooled dramatically the moment we put it up for sale. "Whatever you can afford," she'd said on the phone, and I could tell from the resignation in her voice that she just wanted to be rid of me. She was buying me off. The lawyers would work out the details. Once the transaction was complete, I wouldn't hear from her again.

My legs felt weak as I fiddled with the front gate and approached the house. My old key (I'd been carrying it around for decades) still fit the lock. I remembered to give the door a little nudge at the same time as I twisted the key to unstick the deadbolt, then wiped my shoes on the doormat and stepped inside. The house smelled different, a mustiness having replaced the dense, bready aroma that used to greet me when I came home from school. Most of Dad's things had been put into storage, but the rotary phone remained, wired directly into the house. I picked up the receiver and listened to the dead line, then hung up and went upstairs to inspect the bedrooms. The floorboards creaked under the dingy shag carpet. The doors to both my room and Eileen's were ajar, but Dad's was shut. I gripped the knob and eased it open. His room was just as empty as the rest of the house, the space smaller than I remembered it. I stepped across the threshold and felt strangely embarrassed, as if observing a loved one naked in sleep. I backed out of the room and shut the door.

The bathroom hadn't changed: the pedestal sink, the blue tub. I made sure the water was working, then sat on the edge of the tub. I wouldn't have any furniture for a couple of days. I'd arranged to have Dad's old things delivered to the house later in the week. In the meantime, I would have to sleep on the floor. I took out my smartphone and checked my email. No one had written to me in months. I googled locksmiths and called the first one on the list.

"A1 Security and Locks," a man answered.

"Yes, hello," I said, using the same intonations Dad had always used when conducting business over the phone. "I'm just wondering how soon you can come out to change the locks on my house."

Within days, I'd restored the house to its previous condition, the furniture back where I remembered it, the pictures remounted on the walls, the closets and dressers filled with Dad's old clothes—slightly large, but wearable. When the security company came out, I had them install a state-of-the-art security system with a glowing panel by the front door and discreet video cameras around the perimeter of the house. The following week, I had a landscaping company tear up the front and back lawns, replacing them with no-maintenance rock. I determined exactly what groceries I was going to need and arranged for them to be delivered by the neighbourhood grocer on a weekly basis, the winter shovelling subcontracted out to the grocer's son-in-law. By the time the snow hit the ground, I'd settled in. I paid my last smartphone bill and disconnected my account. All my transactions from that point forward would happen in writing, through the mail.

My plan was to write twelve hours a day. I had a computer, a printer, and a large store of ink and paper. When not at my computer, I read or paced through the house, making a circuit of every level—up and down the stairs, speaking the voices of my characters. The leaps in time stopped, but my sharpened senses gradually began to detect something new: echoes from the past, lingering in the house. The first time I caught a glimpse of Dad walking down the hall with wet hair and a towel around his waist, I'd been terrified, thinking his ghost had come back to haunt me, but when it happened again a few days later, I realized that his movements had been identical, that I was watching a specific moment in time replayed. The following week, I spotted a much younger version of my sister playing on the living room floor with a toddler that it took me a moment to recognize as myself. Before long I was seeing ghosts every day. Eileen and me wrestling on the couch. Dad writing angry letters to the government. Mathilda standing guard at the window. My mother—a shimmering suggestion of a woman—sweeping up and down the stairs. Once I'd grown used to them, these echoes were more consoling than frightening, as I knew that similar echoes must have resonated through Meredith's house; that in spite of everything, I was and always would be back there, lying beside Christine's crib, listening to her soft, regular breaths. But mainly, I tried not to think about the family I'd left behind, focused instead on a new project, a children's book about an orphaned girl named Penelope, who lived under the protection of creatures from another dimension. By the spring, I'd completed the book and immediately began work on a second, with the same protagonist. After some searching, I found a publisher who agreed to print the series, while accepting my two main conditions: that I would write under a pseudonym, and that I would make no public appearances of any kind.

My body fell into its natural rhythm: dropping into unconsciousness when most people woke, waking when most people were coming home from work. I hardly ever looked outside, sliding ever deeper into the worlds I was building for Penelope to explore. Once the books began to appear in print, I had no interest in how well they were doing. The only reader I cared about was Christine. I had my publisher send copies to Meredith in the hopes that she would read them to her out loud, and I personally mailed her as much of the profits as I could spare. I never told Meredith where I'd gone, but she'd clearly found out, as regular letters began to appear in my mailbox: weekly at first, then monthly, and eventually, once a year, around Christmastime. Unable to bring myself to read them, I stuffed the envelopes, unopened, into a shoebox on the fridge.

Time blurred past. An ungodly amount of time. Sometimes I could still feel Christine's sturdy little body against mine, still smell the baby shampoo in her hair. But for the most part, the house did its job and distracted me. I wasn't just seeing the ghosts now, I was hearing them too. Some nights, I could hardly think for the noise: shrieking laughter, monotonous barking, Dad yelling up the stairs, Mother's soft, uncertain voice somewhere at my shoulder. They might not have been aware of me, but I took a voyeuristic, almost godlike pleasure in observing them when they thought they were alone: Dad straining on the toilet, Eileen lip-synching in the mirror, my teenaged self, masturbating furiously in bed.

When the letters from Meredith stopped coming, I assumed the worst, that the end I'd foreseen for Christine had arrived. She was gone. I made an instant chocolate cake on her birthday, covered it with candles, and waited for her ghost to appear. Eventually, seeing nothing but Dad's old kitchen table and three empty chairs, I blew out the candles and threw the cake in the garbage. From that moment on, I stopped keeping track of time, cancelling my newspaper subscription, deliberately averting my gaze from the dates on my written correspondence. But time hadn't forgotten me. Grey threaded its way through my hair and beard, my flesh slackening on the bone, my joints tightening with arthritis. A dozen books into the Penelope series, I couldn't have said just how old I was with any degree of certainty. I was dying, that was all that mattered. I could be patient for this last part. As long as I had royalties, my solitude would be preserved. And for the longest time it was. Then one day, a letter from the postal service informed me of an imminent change. They were, I was told, phasing out the old door-to-door postal system in favour of a more efficient network of community mailboxes, for which I would soon be given a key. My box would be at the end of the block, on the north-east corner of Poplar and Rose (the exact intersection where I'd been struck down as a boy). I had to collect my mail somehow. I was going to have to leave the house.

 I started by stepping out onto the porch, a thin note of terror ringing through my head as I gripped the railing. A few days later, I took one step down the stairs. By the end of the week, I'd made it all the way to the yard, discovering years of accumulated trash and a few resourceful weeds among the rocks. On my next outing, I moved beyond the perimeter of the fence, lurching down the block to snatch a handful of flyers from my assigned cubby. Once a week, I forced myself to make that terrible journey, the peace of mind I'd worked so hard to achieve shattered as I dwelled on small moments from the walk—a child observing me from the passenger window of a slow-moving car, a beautiful young woman saying hello, my disastrous reply. Gradually, the weather began to cool. The leaves changed colour and spiralled to the ground.

 One afternoon, I was standing at the kitchen window by the coffee machine, when a flock of geese passed over the house. My skin tingled as the scene around me grew eerily familiar. I'd eaten breakfast by that same window for years. I'd seen dozens, if not hundreds of geese pass over the house. But there was something about *that* breakfast, *those* geese, the precise quality of light in the window, the way I was holding my cup, that left me feeling I'd experienced the moment before. Only when I burned my mouth and slammed down my cup did my very first trip to the future return to me: the long walk to the bank of mailboxes down the road, the unexpected letter from Meredith.

I leafed through several half-finished books (just as I'd done in my vision), before putting on my shoes. Outside, all the familiar details were there. The wind around my naked ankles. Dad's ghost working on the fence. A boy on a bike. A speeding car. I moved down the sidewalk on a rigid track to the mailbox, not at all surprised to find Meredith's letter in my cubby. I carried it home, spotting Dad's ghost on the roof. My neighbour appeared and I awkwardly saluted her, hauling myself up the front porch, as hail began to fall from the overcast sky.

That was the point where my vision had ended and Christine had jumped into my arms, but now I could follow the story further, into the house. Rather than tearing the letter open immediately, I took down the shoebox with all of Meredith's unopened letters. Judging from the postmarks, she hadn't written in five years. I hadn't seen her in nearly ten. If Christine had still been alive, she would have been twelve years old. Unable to think of anything that Meredith could say that might lessen the pain of that fact, I added her latest letter to the shoebox and went back to the window. The storm had passed. More geese flew over the house, plaintively calling. Next door, the neighbour's lawnmower roared to life. A fist-sized shadow drifted over the rocks in the yard, though I could see nothing to cast it. I went back to the fridge and grabbed the shoebox of letters. Before I could change my mind, I carried the box over to the old woodstove in the living room and shoved it in, lighting a match and setting the whole thing on fire.

CHAPTER EIGHTEEN

A half-dozen empty yellow vehicles sat in a row outside the airport terminal. I stood on the curb with my bag for a long time before an airport employee finally noticed me and came over to explain how the autocabs worked in a loud, patronizing voice, as if I were ninety years old.

"Do you have a device?" he asked.

"I'm sorry?"

"A phone? A wristlet?

"I have a credit card."

He nodded at this quaint, but apparently still functional, technology and pushed a button on the rear hatch, exposing a luggage compartment. I stowed my bag and climbed into the vehicle where, following the man's instructions, I swiped my credit card and told the car where I wanted to go. The autocab signalled and rolled into traffic. At first, I was unnerved by the absence of a driver, but the vehicle inspired confidence, moving more smoothly than any human driver I'd ever encountered. I sat back and looked out the window. Other than this one futuristic change, the city was much as I remembered it. A few new housing developments had sprung up, and most of the larger franchises had been refaced, but the people on the streets were familiar: wealthy retirees and students, tourists and the homeless, all drawn to the coast by the temperate climate. Halfway through the ride, I felt like I'd been using an autocab my whole life, nearly drifting off in the quiet, climate-controlled cab.

At the hotel, I reluctantly stepped back into the world, feeling a bite in the air as I dodged a panhandler and carried my bag into the building. The autocab carried on without me. The lobby was empty. I followed the prominent self-check-in instructions at the front desk, taking my keycard from a slot and pausing at a kiosk beside the elevator to purchase the most basic-looking smartphone on display. It seemed important to have a device in this new world. I toyed with the phone in the elevator, well on my way to making it functional by the time I'd reached my room on the twenty-second floor. I let myself in and flopped onto one of the room's two beds, waking the huge wall-embedded screen before spotting the mini-bar across the room. All the rules I'd been living by for the past decade were tumbling away. Soon a row of small empty bottles stood on the nightstand beside me and I'd immersed myself in a frenetic news cycle dominated by proxy wars and mass killings. Noting a mysterious steel box beside the mini-bar, I pivoted off the bed and pushed to my feet, swaying a little as I opened the box with the help of my new smartphone. Inside, I found a handful of sex toys available for purchase, notably a flashlight-shaped object with a rubberized vagina on one end. Attached to the device were clear instructions for how to synchronize it with the hotel television. With six ounces of hard alcohol in my system, it seemed like the thing to do. Ten minutes later, I was lying on the bed with two pillows under my head, staring at the huge screen in front of me. The device made a low humming noise as it stimulated me in time with the action. It didn't take much imagination to erase the borders around the screen and immerse myself in the experience, with myself as the protagonist and a limber co-ed as my eager partner, but just when my pleasure began to intensify, I caught a glimpse of myself in a mirror across the room—old and exhausted, my cock (which felt slightly bruised) encased in a hard plastic shell. I quickly removed the device and threw it into the garbage, then, reconsidering, wrapped it in a towel and tucked it into my bag. After a long sobering shower, I turned out the lights and went over to the window in my cheap hotel robe. Large, distinct flakes drifted down from the overcast sky. Snow never stayed long on the coast, but on the rare occasions that it came, it fell thick and heavy. I doubted that I would be able to see Meredith's house from there, but looked for it anyway, peering out at the sprawl of the city, isolating one small quadrant, one narrow band, one individual speck of light, which—I became increasingly certain—had been left on just for me. A lantern in a window.

The next morning, I found myself in an idling cab, staring out the window at Meredith's house, her roof covered in two inches of new snow. The driver, a real person who'd briefly tried to make conversation before retreating into offended silence, twisted around to look at me with his elbow on the seat. "Thirty-two fifty," he said flatly.

If I'd been in the autocab, I might have changed my mind and gone straight back to the hotel, but with him staring at me, I felt that I had no choice but to pay and get out of the car. Once he'd gone, I stood in the empty street, looking at the newish SUV in Meredith's driveway. I approached the house slowly, making distinct footsteps in the snow. A pigeon nesting under the gable of a neighbour's roof took to the air with a jackhammer beating of wings, and I came to a brief stop, waiting for someone to shout at me, to demand that I explain my presence. I grabbed the porch railing and climbed, my footfalls on the steps deafening. I touched the doorbell and heard a familiar chime inside. After a few seconds, the deadbolt clunked, and a dangerous swell of emotion rose up in me as the door swung open.

"Oh," Meredith said, in a soft breathless voice.

She was wearing a style of shirt I'd never seen on her before, with a wide collar that flared in the opposite direction that you'd expect. This, more than any physical change, made me aware of the amount of time that had passed since I'd last seen her. "Hello, Meredith," I said, barely holding back the tears. The surprise in her face gave way to concern.

"What are you doing here, Felix?"

"I'm not sure," I admitted.

She looked up and down the street. "Well, you'd better come in. It's freezing."

I followed her into the house, carefully wiping my shoes on the front mat and standing in the entry with my arms at my sides.

"You should have worn a coat," she scolded. Her hands looked different, smaller somehow. She'd repainted in my absence and the furniture was mostly new, but I recognized my old easy chair against the far wall, piled high with papers. I brought my eyes back around in her direction, unable to keep them on her face for long. "Just make yourself at home," she said, a hint of a tremor in her voice. "I'll get some coffee. Do you still drink coffee?"

I nodded.

"Black?"

I nodded again, pleased that she remembered. She disappeared into the kitchen and I walked gingerly through the living room, as if the floor were on fire. An abstract painting hung on the wall opposite the couch—violent sweeps of colour slashing the canvas, like hard-angled rain. I glanced around for Christine's ghost. A low rumble sounded in the kitchen and Meredith stepped back into the living room with two steaming cups. She handed one to me.

"This is quite the surprise," she said, appearing calmer.

"I'm sorry."

"It's all right. It's just...unexpected. You've been getting my letters, then?"

"No," I said. "Well, yes, but I haven't read them."

"I see."

"It was...I just couldn't."

She waved a dismissive hand and sat on a chair a short distance from the couch. A silence fell between us.

"You look good," I finally offered.

She received the compliment with a neutral smile. "How have you been, Felix?"

I couldn't answer, bursting into a half-laugh, half-sob. She waited for me to compose myself, sympathetic but distant.

"Are you on medication?"

I shook my head.

"Do you mind if I ask why not?"

I wiped my eyes with the back of my hand. "As long as I'm alone, I find I can manage."

"So, you live alone."

"Yes."

She nodded, seeming to approve. "I married a few years ago."

"I see," I said weakly.

"I mentioned him in my letters. He's a good man. Not a deep thinker. But he has a big heart."

"Is he..." I said, my voice rising in pitch, "here now?"

"Actually, he's out of town on business. He'll be back tonight."

My eyes drifted around the room, finding no signs of a male presence. "What does he do? Your husband."

"He's a pharmaceutical rep," she said after a slight pause. "He loves Christine very much."

I looked at her sharply, noting her use of the present tense. *Loves.* Beating wings grazed my right ear. The room dimmed and brightened.

"Does he?" I said.

"Yes, he does. He's become like a father to her. I'm sorry, I know that might be hard for you to hear."

"No, no. It's fine. So, Christine..." It hurt just to say her name. "She's..."—I looked at the closed door down the hall—"in her room then?"

"Actually, she slept over at a friend's last night. If I'd have known you were coming..."

I looked around, seeing no more evidence of a twelve-year-old girl in the house than I'd seen of a husband. "What's her name?"

"I'm sorry?"

"Christine's friend. What's her name?"

"Charlotte," Meredith said, her voice tight.

"And what was your husband's name again?"

"Michael." She set down her cup. "You know, I should really give him a call and let him know that—"

"Stop it," I said, abruptly.

"Excuse me?"

"This whole charade. You can stop now."

"I don't know what you're—"

"Why are you acting so nervous?"

"Is that a serious question?" She gave an incredulous laugh. "You show up without warning after all this time. You tell me you're unmedicated. You start asking about Christine's friends..."

I didn't believe her for a moment. At first I'd thought she was trying to protect me, but her insistence on pretending that nothing had happened to Christine had begun to feel malicious. "Let me see her room."

"What?"

"Her room. I want to see it. What did you do with her things? Did you keep them? Or give them away?"

"Felix—"

"I'm not stupid, Meredith. I know what happened. I know that Christine is gone."

"Gone?" Meredith's face softened. "Oh, Felix. What have you been thinking all this time?"

"Stop lying!" I shouted, and at that precise moment, the front door swung open. A chubby girl in a pink bomber jacket and neon toque stepped into the house. Her eyes went between me and Meredith, a silent question in her eyes.

Meredith went pale. "Honey. You're back."

"I forgot my phone."

"Your phone?"

"Yeah. Have you seen it?"

"I don't...I think it might be in your room."

"Okay."

The girl slouched over to her room, staring straight ahead. Her hair was short and some of her features had become more prominent, but it was unmistakably Christine. My baby, resurrected and moving casually (if suspiciously) through the room, close enough to touch. I couldn't tell if she knew who I was. She must have seen photographs, but I'd grown out my hair and beard since leaving, and it might have been enough of a disguise.

"Well," Meredith said, once Christine had closed her door. "I think we were just about finished here, weren't we?"

I heard the warning in her voice and understood what she wanted me to do. I might have found Christine again, but I would not be allowed to keep her. She had adapted to life without me. She had friends. She had *sleepovers*. She had a mom and a stepdad who loved her. They'd carried her this far. They'd kept her safe. I looked at Christine's door, briefly tempted to barge in and reveal myself, but the impulse passed and Meredith must have seen it go, because her face relaxed and she stood up, regarding me with genuine warmth.

"It was good to see you again," she said.

I followed her to the door, where she pressed my hand in gratitude—the first physical contact I'd had in nearly a decade. Muscle and bone. The blood coursing through her veins. I marked that moment, savouring it, promising myself I would return to it often, then turned and made my way down the icy porch. Meredith shut the door behind me. I fished out my new phone. An autocab responded to my pickup request with an estimated arrival time of ten minutes and asked if I wanted to be tracked through the GPS on my phone. I said that I did, and started walking, trusting that they would find me wherever I happened to go.

» » »

On the night Christine was born, I sat by Meredith's side, wondering if I was saying the right things, holding her hand the right way, if the nurses approved or disapproved of my performance. The younger of the two was gorgeous, commanding my helpless gaze whenever she crossed in front of the bed. "Oh!" Meredith said, wincing as another contraction gripped her in its teeth. Teeth, I thought, was the accurate metaphor. She looked like she was being devoured. "Okay," she moaned, reasonably. Then, "Stop-stop-stop-stop-stop," in a strained voice, whether to me or to the creature fighting its way out of her body I couldn't tell.

Her grip on my hand loosened as the contraction passed.

"Good!" the older nurse said in a bright voice, the way a teacher congratulates a student on solving a not-too-difficult math problem. "Wonderful!"

Meredith shut her eyes. I looked at the clock on the wall, my stomach burning with a sudden powerful desire to shit. Her hand spasmed around mine and her eyes snapped open. "No," she said. "Not yet. Oh god—"

The contraction came and went, the old nurse making encouraging noises, while the young one did something with the monitoring equipment, her uniform hugging her generous curves. In a fleeting moment of calmness, Meredith squeezed my hand and smiled at me weakly, gratefully. I tried to smile back, my bowels cramping.

"Do you have any idea how much longer this is going to be?" I asked the old nurse, who ignored me. I lowered my voice to Meredith. "I have to go to the bathroom."

She lay with her eyes closed, in some other place.

"Mer..."

"Just go," the old nurse snapped. The young one looked at me blankly, as if at an empty chair. I slunk over to the room's private bathroom and sat down on the toilet, lowering my head to my hands. It was four in the morning. We'd been at the hospital for nearly sixteen hours. All I wanted to do was sleep. The bathroom fan hummed, drowning out any noise from the adjoining room. I let the shit come, then sat for a while, my eyes shut. The next thing I knew, someone was knocking at the door. "Just a minute!" I yelled, quickly finishing up, before coming out of the bathroom. The scene had changed dramatically in my absence. A doctor had come into the room and was teasing something bloody and awful from between Meredith's legs. For a moment I thought it was the baby, then I noticed Meredith holding something a little more human to her breast—a red, cheesy-looking thing in a pink knit cap. From the clock on the wall, I saw that I'd been gone for more than an hour.

Conscious of the sewer-like smell wafting out from the bathroom behind me, I shut the door and edged over to the bed, past the doctor holding what I assumed to be Meredith's placenta. Meredith looked up at me with a smile.

"She's here," she said hoarsely.

"I'm so sorry."

"About what?"

"I missed everything."

Meredith reached for my hand and gave it a pat. "It's all right."

"I don't know what happened."

"It's fine."

The baby gazed steadily at Meredith as she fed. If I'd have left the room at that moment, she would have never known who I was, what I looked like, what it felt like to be held by me. What it meant to lose me. The doctor had carted the placenta off somewhere and the nurses were tidying up the mess between Meredith's legs.

"You should hold her," Meredith said.

My eyes filled with tears. I didn't want her. I didn't deserve her. I worried that by touching her, I would ruin her, infect her with my sickness. But looking at her ancient little face, and her big dark eyes, I felt the first hooks of tenderness lodge into my heart. I was lost. Meredith handed me the swaddled heap as the old nurse watched on with a stern eye, and the young nurse turned down the lights. The baby regarded me solemnly. I slipped a protective hand behind her head as I'd been shown, and she fussed for a moment, then settled as I began to rock her with a motion that came from some primal place. Meredith watched us with a fond smile. Even the old nurse seemed pleased.

Standing at the hotel window twelve years later, I'd fallen into that same comforting rhythm. Another wave of heavy snow had begun to fall, obscuring my view of the street. I pictured my replacement arriving home from his business trip, Meredith looking over with relief as his key slid into the lock, Christine coming out of her room to ask, *Is Dad home?*

Light exploded in my eyes. I fell back and felt the solid support of a forearm rise to meet me. My mother's smiling face swung into view. She lowered me to her breast, humming softly, her face suffused with tenderness. I fed without reservation, without shame, struggling to hold her there in front of me, but my eyes were growing heavy with the gentle rocking of her body, and before I knew what was happening, I'd fallen asleep.

My flight home was delayed on account of the snow. With a few minutes to spare, I wandered the length of the terminal, ending up in the gift shop, where I came to their small collection of children's books, surprised to see the latest installment in the Penelope series prominently featured. I picked it up with a mixture of pride and embarrassment. The cover depicted Penelope riding the back of her friend and protector, Swell, a large, hummingbird-like creature, through a wormhole into the future, her eyes bright with exaggerated joy. She looked nothing like Christine. I put the book down and quickly left the store.

It was getting late. By the time I found my gate, the other passengers had boarded. An unsmiling host directed me down a short hallway to the waiting aircraft, and I followed my ticket to a window seat near the back of the plane. There was hardly anyone on board, my entire row empty. A flight attendant in a pantsuit glided down the aisle, her long red hair in a bun, her face in shadow. She passed into business class and a heavy curtain fell shut behind her. The cabin lights dimmed. Dread spiked through me as I heard them lock the door up front, but the feeling quickly passed, as if a light sedative had been introduced into the ventilation system. Outside, a marshaller in a toque and reflective vest made what looked like the sign of the cross, directing us over to a row of yellow trucks that stood waiting, like pallbearers on the edge of a snowy field. One detached from the group, lifting an operator in an enclosed basket to the level of my window. Nozzles stroked the wing, swabbing it, as one swabs a vein prior to an injection. The operator met my eye and looked away.

Once the wings had been de-iced, the yellow truck retreated to a respectful distance, and the plane began to taxi again, guided by a single track of lights that stretched out as far as I could see. Finally, we came to a stop, and there was a drawn-out moment of stillness. I felt like I should lower my head and pray. The engine noise swelled to a deafening pitch. Then we were moving again, with purpose, rapidly picking up speed, the clouds rushing towards us in a dark flood. I gripped my armrests, waiting for the moment when the wheels left the ground, but it happened in one seamless breath. The plane rose quickly, as if untethered from the world, the city briefly rendered in miniature beneath us until we passed, shuddering through the clouds. The upper element was jarringly serene. From above, the clouds appeared solid, as if we might land on them. A band of pink flared at the western horizon, signalling the arrival of dusk. I took out my smartphone and stared at its blank face for a moment, the battery dead. The red-haired flight attendant failed to reappear. I put my phone away and looked up and down the aisle, unable to see any of my fellow passengers.

A soft chime sounded as the captain activated the intercom, allowing a prolonged hissing silence to gather. I had the sense of being judged, the whole of my life held up on a little strip of tape. Out the window, a single bird skimmed the roof of the clouds. The stars began to reveal themselves. Still the captain did not speak. The silence went on and on—a maddening, baffling blankness onto which I could have projected any number of feelings: boredom, amusement, pity, disgust.

Even love.

ACKNOWLEDGMENTS

I would like to thank the Saskatchewan Arts board for their support with this project. Thank you to everyone at Freehand Books, and especially Deborah Willis for thinking of me. Thanks to Sarah Feldman for her early work on the manuscript, and to Rosemary Nixon for her incisive line editing. Thank you to Grandma K. for her babysitting services and to Pearl Z. for her generosity. Finally, thank you to my children and my wife Rebecca, without whom I would be lost.

Devin Krukoff's previous novels, *Compensation* and *Flyways*, were shortlisted for multiple Saskatchewan Book Awards. He is a past winner of the M&S Journey Prize for short fiction. He lives in Regina, Saskatchewan, with his family.